Witch Is How
The Mirror Lied

Published by Implode Publishing Ltd
© Implode Publishing Ltd 2018

Chapter 1

"This is empty." Jack waved the muesli box under my nose.

"Why are you telling me? I'm not the muesli fairy. You should have called at the corner shop on your way home last night."

"I forgot. Couldn't you just—" He gave me a sickly-sweet smile. "You know."

"What?"

"Magic some for me."

"What about our no-magic pact?"

"I only need enough for one bowlful."

"Are you asking me to break a solemn promise just so you can have muesli for breakfast?"

"Yes." He gave me a peck on the cheek. "Pretty please."

"Okay, then." I closed my eyes and cast the spell. "There you go. It's in the box."

"Thanks, gorgeous. You're my favourite witch."

Not for long, I suspected.

I hurried out of the kitchen, and had made it halfway up the stairs when he shouted.

"Hey! This is sawdust!"

Snigger.

"I suppose you think that was funny," he said, when I came back downstairs ten minutes later. "I might have eaten that."

"You probably wouldn't have noticed any difference. Hey, did I tell you the replacement sign is being installed this morning?"

"Do you think they'll get it right this time?"

"They'd better. I'm fed up with people asking if you've decided to come and work with me."

"Actually, that's not a bad idea. We'd make a great team."

"If we worked together, we'd be divorced within a year."

"You're probably right. I'm not sure I could adjust to your way of working."

"What do you mean by that?"

"You're not exactly organised. It's all pretty much by the seat of your pants, isn't it?"

"It may appear chaotic to you, but I'll have you know that it all works like a well-oiled machine."

"If you say so. You haven't forgotten that I'm away again on Sunday, have you?"

"You're never here."

"I can't help it. These courses are like buses: There are none for ages and then they all come at once."

"What's this one about?"

"I can't remember—something deadly boring. I'd rather stay here—I was rather looking forward to the Clownathon. You'll have to take photos."

"What makes you think I'm going?"

"Oh yes, I'd forgotten that you're terrified of clowns."

"Why does everyone keep saying that? I'm not scared of them; it's just that I find them boring."

"That's not what Kathy told me."

"You should know by now not to take any notice of anything my sister says."

"She reckons you used to hide behind the sofa whenever they came on TV."

At that moment, there was a knock at the door.

"It's probably clowns." Jack laughed.

"You'd better answer it, then, seeing as you reckon I'm so scared of them."

"It's the fish man," Jack shouted from the hallway.

Fishman? Didn't I have enough to contend with already with sups and ghosts? I didn't need to add superheroes to the mix.

"What does he want?" I went to join Jack at the door.

"Take a wild guess." Jack stood to one side so that I could see the white van parked at the end of the drive. On its side were pictures of fish and shellfish, and the words: The Fish Man.

"Morning, love, sorry to call on you so early, but I'm trying to catch people before they go to work. I'm Terry. Terry Salmon."

If this man was a superhero, his outfit, a plain white coat, sucked big time.

"Terry is starting a delivery round," Jack said.

"I used to have a shop in Washbridge, but the rent and rates were killing me, so I decided to go mobile."

"That's very nice, but we buy all of our fish from the local chippy."

"Tish and Chip?" Jack scoffed. "It's hardly the same thing. Terry is selling freshly caught fish, delivered direct to the door. And he sells a much wider range too."

"That's true," Terry chipped in. "As well as all the usual favourites: Cod, haddock, plaice and what-have-you, I have lots of other species. Shellfish too."

"I do enjoy the occasional mussel," Jack said. "And prawns."

"Prawns are my speciality." Terry obviously sensed that

he had Jack on the hook. "Can I add you to my list? I plan to call around once a week."

"Do you sell soft furnishings too?" I asked.

"Sorry?"

"Tish and Chip do a nice range of curtains and cushions."

"Ignore her." Jack shot me a look. "She's *clowning* around. Please go ahead and add our name to your list."

"Great. See you soon, then."

The Fish Man had taken his leave, and Jack and I were back in the kitchen.

"What was that all about?" I said. "I've never seen anyone get so excited about fish as you just did."

"I love shellfish. It's ages since I had scallops."

"Scallops are gross. Anyway, isn't it time you were leaving? You said you had to be at work early this morning."

"Oh cripes, is that the time? Why didn't you tell me?"

"I couldn't get a word in edgeways for all the fish talk."

"See you tonight." He gave me a kiss, and then sprinted for the door. I expected to hear it slam closed behind him, but instead I heard him talking to someone. I assumed that Fish Man must have forgotten something, but then Jack shouted, "Kathy's here! Go on through, Kathy. Sorry, I have to dash."

Kathy walked into the kitchen. "Jack seems to be in a hurry."

"He was supposed to go into work early, but he was so busy going on about fish that he forgot."

"Don't tell me he's into fishing now, too?"

"Not catching them; eating them. We've had a visit

from Fish Man, and before you ask, no he isn't a superhero. His name is Terry Salmon, and he's started to run a mobile fishmonger service."

"Really? I wonder if he's going to cover our area too? Pete and I both love a nice piece of haddock."

"Don't you start. There's been enough fish talk in this house for one day. What are you doing here, anyway?"

"A cup of tea would be nice."

"It'll have to be quick. Some of us have work to go to."

"I'm going in later, but I wanted to have a quick word with you about Lizzie first."

"Is she okay?" I put the kettle on.

"Yeah. Well, I think so. She's been talking even more about ghosts recently. I don't know what I should do about it. I keep hoping it's a phase she's going through, and that one day she'll forget all about it."

"Is it upsetting her?"

"No, quite the contrary. She's never been happier."

"Well then. I wouldn't worry."

"You're probably right. When she's a teenager, and she gets interested in boys, I'll no doubt be wishing that she was back in this phase."

"Would you like me to have a chat with her?"

"No, it's okay. I'm being silly."

I poured us both a cup of tea and we sat at the kitchen table.

"No biscuits?" She pouted.

"I'm all out."

"Liar." She went over to the cupboard and grabbed my last packet of custard creams.

"Don't eat them all. They have to last me all week."

"These won't last you the day." She managed to take

two before I snatched the packet away from her. "By the way, who have you been upsetting around here?"

"What do you mean?"

"Haven't you seen the graffiti on the toll bridge?"

"What graffiti?"

"It probably isn't anything to do with you anyway." She took a sip of tea. "There must be more than one Jill around here. It's probably kids who did it."

"What exactly does it say?"

"Jill is a witch."

I almost spat out my tea. "When did you see it?"

"Just now, on my way here. It reminded me of what your birth mother said that day in the nursing home."

"Sorry?" I was barely listening to her—I was too busy trying to process what she'd said about the graffiti.

"Don't you remember her dying words to you? She called you a witch."

"Oh yeah, I'd forgotten about that. Like you said, it's probably kids." I drank the rest of my tea. "I really do have to get going."

"Okay. Pete told me I shouldn't worry about Lizzie, but it's hard not to sometimes. He's more concerned about the central heating."

"Has it packed up?"

"No, it's still working, but it's not as effective as it used to be. Certain rooms are always cold—our bedroom in particular. I think we're going to have to get someone to come out and take a look at it."

A few minutes after Kathy had left, I set off for the office.

The graffiti on the toll bridge must have been put up

overnight, or I would have seen it on my way home the previous evening. Giant red letters spelled out the words: JILL IS A WITCH.

Kathy was right, there had to be other women called Jill living in and around Smallwash, but there was no doubt in my mind that it was aimed at me.

The young man in the toll booth was still persevering in his attempt to grow a moustache. It now resembled an underfed caterpillar clinging to the bottom of his nose.

""Excuse me, young man. Do you know who put up the graffiti?"

"No idea. I didn't start until six this morning. It was already there then."

"What about the guy who worked the nightshift? Did he say anything about it when he handed over to you?"

"No. Gordy didn't even know it was there until I pointed it out to him. It's dead quiet in the early hours of the morning—they probably did it while he'd dozed off."

"Has anyone reported it?"

"I called head office when I got here. They said they'd get around to it when they could." He scratched the caterpillar. "You're not *Jill*, are you? The witch?"

"Me? No. I just think it's an eyesore, that's all."

***

I'd parked the car, and was walking towards the office when I spotted that the sign had already been changed. Not before time too.

Hold on! What the—?

I dashed upstairs, and crashed into the outer office.

"Have you seen the sign?"

"I'm sorry, Jill," Mrs V said. "There was nothing I could do about it. They must have been here at the crack of dawn because it was already up when I arrived."

"*Jill* and *Max Well*? What is wrong with that man? It's not like I didn't spell it out for him."

"Normally, I would have been here in time to stop them, but Armi has started to give me driving lessons. He's going to let me drive to work and back each day. This morning was my first one."

"How did it go?"

"Alright. I keep flashing at the wrong time, but other than that, I seem to be doing okay. Do you want me to give Mr Song a call?"

"No, I think I should speak to him myself. There is something you can do, though. Will you see if you can find any companies that specialise in removing graffiti, please?"

"I didn't see any graffiti on my way in."

"It isn't on this building."

"Don't tell me someone has vandalised your house?"

"No. It's on the toll bridge on the way into Smallwash."

"Isn't that the bridge operator's responsibility?"

"Probably, but you know how long it can take for these organisations to sort things out, and it's a real eyesore."

"I have to say, Jill, that's very public-spirited of you."

"I like to do my bit."

"That sign of yours is the joke that keeps on giving." Winky was practically in tears.

"I'm glad you're amused."

"*Well*, I do intend milking it to the *max*." He rolled onto his side. "Get it? *Well? Max?*"

"I'm not in the mood for your pathetic jokes."

He eventually managed to compose himself. "I'm guessing this isn't a good time to discuss the state of this office?"

"What are you talking about?"

"Do you remember I was having dinner with Crystal on Saturday?"

"Oh yeah, the blind date. How did it go?"

"Very well, as it happens, but she—err—well, she wasn't overly impressed by this office."

"Do you seriously think I care what this week's girlfriend thinks about my office?"

"Crystal is not *this week's* girlfriend, as you put it. In fact, I see a long future ahead for the two of us."

"Not if you three-time her like you did with the last batch."

"Crystal is different."

"What exactly did she say was wrong with my office, anyway? Not that I care."

"Look around; it's a dump. Those blinds have been stuck like that for years, your desk is on its last legs, and this wooden floor needs treating. Oh, and that sofa has seen better days."

"If you don't like living here, you know where the door is."

"I thought you were all about image and marketing nowadays?"

"I am."

"What's the point of attracting prospective clients if they're going to be put off as soon as they walk through that door?"

"I suppose it wouldn't do any harm to get a quote for some new blinds."

"What about that awful desk?"

"I love this desk. No way am I getting rid of this."

"The sofa, then. Look at the state of it."

"You're the only one who uses it."

"All the more reason to get a new one."

"I'll consider it if you go halves."

"I'm just a cat. I don't have any money."

"Don't give me that old rubbish. I've lost count of all the money-making schemes you've got on the go. You can afford to stump up half."

"I doubt the Cats Protection League would be impressed if they knew you were making me pay."

"Why don't you go and tell them, then?"

"I've said it before, and I'll say it again—you've changed since you got married."

Chapter 2

"No, Mr Song, I did not say *Jill* and *Max Well*. It's just Jill."

"What happened to Max?" Sid said, in his usual singsong manner.

"Nothing has happened to *Max*—there never was a *Max*. It's just me; I changed my name from Jill Gooder to Jill Maxwell when I got married recently."

"Congratulations."

"Thanks, but we went through all of this when you installed the first incorrect sign."

"I can only apologise, but I did have a bit of a tumble, you know."

"Yes, and I was sorry to hear about that, but my understanding was that you injured your ankle. I'm not sure that explains this second mix up."

"You're right. It shouldn't have happened."

"You'll get it sorted, then?"

"Of course."

"And there'll be no charge?"

"Certainly not. It was my mistake."

"When can I expect the replacement sign?"

"I'll get on it as soon as I come back from my holiday."

"*Holiday*? When are you going?"

"As soon as I've finished on this call. You were lucky to catch me—I only popped in to pick up the post. Me and Cissie, that's the wife, are off to Ibiza. In fact, I'd better get going or we'll miss our flight."

"Hold on. How long will you be gone for?"

"A couple of weeks."

"And you'll get straight onto this as soon as you get

back?"

"Of course. It'll be my first job."

"And you definitely know what I want this time: Jill Maxwell. Nothing else."

"Got it. Sorry, I have to dash. Cissie is tooting the horn."

"Please make sure—"

Too late—he'd hung up.

"You really told him." Winky grinned.

"Can it, you. I'm not in the mood."

"You could always tell people that I'm Max if anyone asks."

"One more quip from you and there'll be no salmon for a week."

Mrs V popped her head around the door. "Did you manage to sort out the sign, dear?"

"Kind of, but Sid is going on holiday, so we're stuck with this one for a couple of weeks."

"What will I do if someone asks for Max?"

"They won't."

"But if they do?"

"Tell them that Max has retired and it's just me now."

"As you wish, dear. Oh, and I managed to get hold of someone who can clean up the graffiti."

"Good. What did they say?"

"He was a very nice man. I think he said his name is Mr Tatts. As luck would have it, he's working on a job in Washbridge this morning, so he said he could come in and see you in an hour or two. I hope that's okay?"

"That's great. It'll give me time to pop out for a coffee."

"I could make you one."

"It's okay. I could do with stretching my legs."

"What's with the graffiti?" Winky asked when Mrs V had gone back to her desk.

"Someone has sprayed it on the toll bridge near Smallwash."

"Why would you care about that?"

"Because they wrote: Jill is a witch."

"It sounds like someone has it in for you."

"It might not even be aimed at me. Maybe it's another Jill. Maybe someone doesn't like her and decided to call her a witch."

"And maybe I'll be elected prime minister next week."

"People do sometimes use the term 'witch' as an insult. When my birth mother told me I was a witch, I thought she was just being horrible to me."

"You must think it's aimed at you otherwise you wouldn't be paying someone to remove it."

"I'm playing it safe."

"If you say so. Anyway, I've had a brilliant idea about the sign."

"I don't want to hear it. I'm going for a coffee."

***

This definitely wasn't the start to the new week that I'd been hoping for. Maybe coffee and a muffin would cheer me up. On my way down to Coffee Games, there were posters advertising the Clownathon on practically every lamppost. I was secretly quite pleased that Jack would be away on a course on Sunday, otherwise he would no doubt have tried to drag me there.

"Morning!" The bubbly young witch behind the counter was obviously a new recruit. Nothing else could have explained that degree of enthusiasm. "I'm Sarah."

"Hi. Jill."

"I'm really glad you came in," she said, in little more than a whisper. "You're the first sup I've seen in here so far. I was beginning to worry."

"When did you start working here?"

"Only this morning, but I thought I might have had a few sups through the door by now."

"To be honest, there are never many sups in here. I'm not sure why. The prices are a bit steep—maybe that's it."

"It's my first time working in the human world, so I'm a little nervous."

"You'll be fine. Are you living in Washbridge?"

"Not at the moment. I magic myself back and forth, to and from Candlefield every day. I thought I'd see how it goes before renting somewhere over here."

"That's sensible."

"What can I get for you, Jill?"

"Can I get a caramel latte and—err—I don't normally indulge, but I think I'll have one of those blueberry muffins, please."

What? Who are you to judge? Don't think I can't see you with that giant slab of cake in your hand.

"There you go." She handed me the drink and muffin. "What do you do in Washbridge, Jill, if you don't mind my asking?"

"I'm a private investigator. My offices are just off the high street."

"I think I know where you mean—I saw them putting up your sign this morning. Do you have a partner called

Max?"

Oh boy.

"No, actually it's just me. There was a mix up with the sign."

"I see." She obviously didn't, but I didn't have the energy to try to explain. "Do you want a mousetrap, Jill?"

"Why? Have you got mice in here?" I glanced around the floor.

"No." She laughed. "I meant the game. It's Mouse Trap day today."

"Oh, right. No, I'm okay, thanks. I'll only be here for a few minutes."

"Nice to meet you, Jill." She moved down the counter to serve another customer.

***

On my way back into the office building, I bumped into Lucas Morecake and his partner — the delightful Wendy. They'd recently opened an escape room in what had previously been I-Sweat. Lucas was usually happy-go-lucky, but this morning he looked like a man with the weight of the world on his shoulders.

"Lucas. Wendy. How are you both? How's business?"

"Fine." Wendy snapped. As charming as ever.

"Actually, we have a bit of a prob—" Lucas began.

"Come on, Lucas." Wendy grabbed him by the arm, and practically dragged him upstairs.

"Is everything okay?" I called after them, but they'd already disappeared down the corridor.

"These two *ladies* would like to see you, Jill." Mrs V

gestured to the two old dears seated near the wool basket. They looked vaguely familiar, but I couldn't think why. "I told them that you might not be able to see them without an appointment."

"Myrtle asked us to come and see you," the taller of the two women said.

It was only then that I realised where I knew them from. They were Myrtle Turtle's sidekicks: Hodd and Jobbs.

"Is Myrtle alright?"

"She's in a spot of bother, actually." Hodd glanced at Mrs V and then back at me. "Could we speak in private?"

"Of course. Come through to my office."

"Would either of you two *ladies* care for a drink?" Mrs V offered, somewhat reluctantly.

"Do you have any of the hard stuff?" Jobbs said.

"You're supposed to be off the drink, remember?" Hodd admonished her. "I'll have a coffee: black, very strong and no sugar."

Jobbs sighed. "I suppose I'll have to have the same then, seeing as how I'm not allowed a proper drink. Five sugars for me, though."

"Five?" Mrs V looked horrified.

"Yeah, I've decided to cut back. Apparently, it's not good for you."

"Two black coffees it is, then. What about you, Jill?"

"I'm okay, thanks, Mrs V. I've had one at Coffee Games."

"He's a handsome fellow, and no mistake." Hodd walked over to Winky who was lying on the sofa. "He reminds me of Old Tom."

"Is Old Tom your cat?"

"Nah. The last time I was detained at Her Majesty's Pleasure, Old Tom used to come and beg scraps from us in the exercise yard. It was supposed to be a high-security gaff, and no one could figure out how he got in and out, but he was there twice a day, regular as clockwork. He looked just like your boy here except that Old Tom only had one ear." She reached down to pick Winky up.

"Don't bring that thing over here!" Jobbs yelled at her. "No offence, Jill, but I'm allergic to cat hair, as Hodd knows only too well."

"Sorry, boy." Hodd gave him a stroke instead. Winky was lapping up the attention, and had his purr set to max volume.

"Hodd, leave that cat alone, and come over here." Jobbs patted the seat next to her. "Have you forgotten that Turtle is in the nick?"

"What?" I was gobsmacked. "Myrtle is in prison?"

"Only on remand." Hodd joined us at the desk.

"On what charge?"

"Murder."

Before I could react, Mrs V appeared with the coffee. "Black, strong and no sugar."

"Thanks." Hodd took the cup from her.

"And black, strong and *five* sugars for you."

"Thanks." Jobbs took hers. "You're a sweetheart."

"You'd better tell me what happened." I had to raise my voice in order to be heard over Jobbs' slurping. For reasons known only to her, she'd poured some of the coffee into the saucer, and was drinking it from there.

"They found Rob Evans dead, downstream from the watermill," Hodd said. "They thought he'd drowned at first, but it turned out that someone had given him a crack over the head before he went into the water."

"Was Rob Evans a resident of Middle Tweaking?"

"Yeah, but he only moved in recently. He inherited his grandmother's place after she died. Josie was a little old darling, but Rob is—err—*was* a complete waste of space."

"He'd been holding wild parties." Jobbs had finished her coffee. "He invited all kinds of people into the village—lots of them were drunk or worse. And then there was the loud music until all hours. Most people were too afraid to say anything, but not Turtle. She went in all guns blazing, and told him to show some respect for his neighbours."

"It didn't do much good, though," Hodd said. "He was still having at least one party a week up until the time someone put an end to it."

"Killed him, you mean?" I said. "You surely don't think it was Myrtle?"

"Course not." Hodd put her empty cup on my desk. "Turtle's a tough old bird, but she wouldn't murder anyone."

"Why have they got her locked up, then?"

"It's the Old Bill. They don't know their backside from their elbow, as usual."

"I thought she and Sergeant Cross were friends."

"They were—still are. But Charlie had to retire some months ago on health grounds. The woman they brought in to replace him is a proper cow."

"Her name is Rosemary Thorne," Jobbs said. "She's young and ambitious. The only thing she's interested in his her clear-up rate."

"Still, she wouldn't arrest Myrtle without some

evidence, surely?"

"As far as we can make out, they're basing their case on circumstantial evidence. Myrtle managed to get word out to us through her solicitor. She said if anyone could get her out, you could. Will you help?"

"Of course. I'll need to speak to Myrtle. Do you think that can be arranged?"

"I would think so." Jobbs stood up. "We'll have a word with her solicitor, and get back to you."

"What do you call this handsome guy?" Hodd walked back over to Winky, and started to stroke him again.

"Winky — on account of his missing eye."

"If you ever get fed up with him, I'll take him off your hands."

"No, you won't," Jobbs started for the door. "Not unless you want me to move out."

"That would be a bonus." Hodd grinned. "Thanks for your time, Jill. We'll let you know once the prison visit has been arranged."

"I like her," Winky said, once the odd couple had left. "I don't think much to her buddy, though."

"They're a very strange couple."

"How do you know them? Were you inside with them?"

"No, I wasn't! I've never been in prison. Not for more than a few hours, anyway."

"That old Turtle bird came here once, didn't she? If I remember correctly, she took a real shine to me."

"Yeah, but I won't hold that against her. And I'm not sure she'd appreciate you referring to her as an old bird."

"I didn't have her down as a murderer."

"Neither did I. Hopefully, this is all some silly misunderstanding."

Chapter 3

Mrs V popped her head around my door. "The man is here about the graffiti, Jill. He's picking out a pair of socks, then I'll send him through, shall I?"

"Yes, please."

"It's not every day a client gives me a free pair of socks." The man held them aloft. "I chose these, what do you think?"

"That's a nice shade of green. I'm Jill Maxwell. Please have a seat. My PA said your name was Mr Tatts, I believe?"

"Not exactly." He laughed and gestured to his arms, which were covered in tattoos. "The name's Jim Brown but everyone calls me Tatts, for obvious reasons."

"I appreciate you coming to see me at such short notice."

"No problem; I was in town anyway. I didn't notice any graffiti on my way into the building."

"Actually, the graffiti isn't here. Do you happen to know the toll bridge on the road to Smallwash?"

"Yeah, my sister lives out that way."

"The graffiti is on the bridge."

"Look, I'm grateful for the work, but isn't it their responsibility to get it removed?"

"Strictly speaking, yes, but you know how long these things can take. I'd like it gone quickly; today if possible."

"What is it, exactly?"

"It's the only graffiti on that bridge, so you can't miss it. It says: Jill is a witch."

"It sounds like someone has it in for you. Do you know

who did it?"

"No, and I can't even be sure that it's aimed at me, but I'd like it removed anyway."

"Fair enough. It doesn't sound like a big job, and I've nothing else on for the rest of the day, so I could go straight over there. How does one hundred and seventy-five pounds sound?"

"That'll be fine, provided you can do it today."

"I'll get straight onto it." He stood up. "Thanks again for the socks."

"You ought to get a tattoo," Winky said, after Tatts had left.

"I don't think so."

"You could have one of me, on your arm or ankle."

"I'm not a big fan of tattoos, but if I ever do have one, it certainly won't be one of you."

"Your loss. Anyway, his visit has given me an idea."

"Let me guess. You're going to set up your own graffiti removal service?"

"Nah, that sounds too much like hard work. I was thinking that I could start a little sideline, as a tattoo artist. I have quite an artistic flair, you know."

"No one in their right mind is going to trust a cat to give them a tattoo."

"I wouldn't be aiming my services at you two-leggeds. I'm talking about providing tattoos for felines."

"I think you're forgetting something. Cats have fur. Duh!"

"You know nothing about felines, do you?"

"I know that most cats have fur, so they can't have tattoos."

"You've obviously never heard of fur patches?"

"Of what?"

"Humans aren't the only ones who like tattoos. Cats do too. That's why someone came up with the idea of fur patches. Obviously, felines have to be discreet when they're around two-leggeds because they'd be freaked out if they found their darling cat had a tattoo. That's where the fur patch comes in."

"So how does this patch work exactly?"

"It allows the cat to have a section of fur removed where the tattoo will be located. When the cat is among other felines, the tattoo can be on display, but when it's with two-leggeds, it's hidden by the fur patch."

"That's the most ridiculous thing I've ever heard."

"Don't blame me; I don't write this stuff. Anyway, the point is there's a big demand for tattoos among the feline population, and I expect to make a killing."

***

These days, I didn't often get the chance to see Aunt Lucy by herself because, Tuesday through to Friday, she looked after one of the babies, so that the twins could work in Cuppy C. As Monday was her day off from her babysitting duties, I decided to pay her a visit.

"Hi, Jill." She was in the kitchen, and whatever she was baking smelled delicious. "Cup of tea?"

"That would be lovely. What are you making?"

"Just a few cupcakes."

"Mmm, yummy."

"They won't be ready for a while yet, I'm afraid, but there is a new packet of custard creams in the cupboard."

She filled the kettle while I got the biscuits.

"Are you enjoying your day off, Aunt Lucy?"

"It doesn't feel right to call it a *day off*. I love having the babies here."

"They must be hard work, though?"

"Of course, but I don't mind. They won't be babies for very long, as I know only too well, so I intend to enjoy them while I can."

"You won't know what to do with yourself when they start at nursery."

"Maybe I'll have another baby to look after by then." She grinned.

"Mine? I don't think so."

"You and Jack do want children one day, don't you?"

"It's not something we've talked about yet. We're only just getting used to being married."

She poured the tea, and then we went through to the lounge. We'd no sooner sat down than I heard the unmistakable pounding of paws on the stairs.

"I thought we were doing well." Aunt Lucy smiled.

I'd just managed to put my cup on the coffee table before Barry launched himself at me.

"Steady on, boy. It doesn't usually take you this long to come and say hello. I thought you must be out with Dot."

"I was waiting for Rhymes to finish writing my poem." Barry raised his head, so I could see the small slip of paper tucked into his collar. "Read it, Jill! It's all about me."

"Okay." I grabbed the paper.

Barry is a dog who likes to please,
He's big and fluffy and doesn't have fleas,
His favourite things are Barkies and going for a walk,
He doesn't have a lot to say, but boy can that dog talk.

"Isn't it brilliant, Jill?" Barry was spinning around in circles with excitement.

"It — err — certainly captures the essence of who you are."

"What's *essence*?"

"It means that it sums you up very well."

"Rhymes says I should make up a poem about him."

"That's a good idea. You should go for it."

"I can't write, though."

"You could still make up a poem in your head."

"How would I do that?"

"Think of what you want to say, and keep the words in your memory. Do you think you could do that?"

"I can try. Can we go for a walk now? I love going for a walk."

"Dot's coming to collect you in a few minutes," Aunt Lucy said. "Have you forgotten?"

"And Babs?"

"Yes, Dot's taking you and Babs out for a walk in the park."

"I love the park! I love Babs! And I love going for a walk."

Just then, there was a knock at the door.

"That'll be her."

Barry charged out of the room, and the next thing I heard was the sound of his paws hitting the front door.

It was ages since I'd seen Dot, but I didn't get the chance to say more than a quick hello because the two dogs were eager to be on their way.

"How are you coping with Rhymes?" I asked, once Aunt Lucy and I were alone again.

"He's no trouble, but the poetry thing does get a bit much sometimes."

"You'll get a break when he hibernates."

"I'm afraid not. Animals don't hibernate here in Candlefield. Not like they do in the human world."

"I didn't know that."

"Hiya, Mum!"

"We're here!"

The twins shouted from the hallway, and then came charging through to the lounge.

"Looks like we've timed it right." Amber grabbed the armchair closest to the sofa. "I'm gagging for a cup of tea."

"Something smells nice." Pearl propped herself on the arm of the same chair.

"You're out of luck. The cupcakes won't be ready for ages yet. It's just custard creams unless Jill has eaten them already." Aunt Lucy stood up. "I'll go and pour you two some tea."

"Thanks, Mum."

"Yeah, thanks, Mum."

"Where are the babies?" I said.

"We came up with a brilliant plan." Amber leaned forward in the chair. "Didn't we, Pearl?"

"Yeah, we talked the guys into changing their shifts around so that they can be off on Mondays. It means that we can spend more time together as a family."

"So, how come you're here now without them?"

"We thought it would be a good idea if we let the guys have some one-on-one time with the kids. Just for this first week. And, anyway, we know that Mum gets lonely sometimes, so we thought we'd pay her a visit."

"That was very thoughtful of them, wasn't it, Jill?" Aunt Lucy brought cups of tea through for the twins. "To think of their old Mum like that?"

"Very."

"Well, this is all very cosy." Grandma appeared in the doorway.

"Hello, Mother." Aunt Lucy had been about to sit down. "I suppose you'll want a cup of tea, too?"

"If it isn't too much bother. I wouldn't want to impose."

"It's no bother at all." Aunt Lucy disappeared back into the kitchen.

"The things I have to put up with." Grandma grumbled as she came and sat next to me. It was obvious that she wanted us to ask what was troubling her, but the twins and I knew better. Of course, that didn't stop her from telling us anyway. "And it's all the fault of that sister of yours."

"Kathy? What's she done?"

"She keeps stealing my ideas and using them in her shop."

"I very much doubt that. Kathy is more than capable of coming up with her own ideas."

"Says you."

"She must be doing something right because she's talking about opening another shop in West Chipping."

"Do I look like I care? And as for that nasty little assistant of hers—"

"May?"

"Whatever her name is. She's downright rude."

"May has always been perfectly polite to me."

"She told me to sling my hook the other day."

"What were you doing?"

"Nothing. Just looking around their shop."

"Stealing Kathy's ideas, you mean?"

"Nonsense. I don't need to steal ideas from that amateur."

"Kathy told me that's precisely what you've been doing. She's probably given May instructions to keep a lookout for you."

"If that young woman thinks she can speak to me like that, she has another think coming."

"Don't do anything silly, Grandma."

"Here, Mother." Aunt Lucy passed Grandma a cup of tea. "This will help to calm you down."

"I don't want to calm down." She took the tea anyway. "I don't mind a little fair competition, but that sister of Jill's is underhanded."

"That's rich, coming from you." I scoffed. "You'll do anything to crush the competition."

She took a slurp of tea. "Anyway, where are my great-grandchildren? It's ages since I saw them."

"They're with William and Alan," Amber said.

"Who are they?"

"You know very well who they are, Mother." Aunt Lucy sighed. "They're the twins' husbands."

"I can't be expected to remember everyone's name. When do I get to see the two Bills, then?"

"They're little girls, Mother, and their names are Lil and Lily."

"So? When do I get to see them?"

"They're here with me every Tuesday, Wednesday, Thursday and Friday. All you have to do is walk around from next door."

"And they're little girls, you say? Are you sure? I could have sworn they were boys."

"They're definitely little girls. I've changed their nappies enough times to be sure of that."

***

On my drive home, I saw Tatts on the toll bridge. He was already well on with the work; all that remained of the offending graffiti were the words: A WITCH.

I pulled up alongside him.

"It looks like it's coming off okay."

"Hi there. Yeah, it's no problem. I should be done in another thirty minutes or so."

I was surprised to find Jack's car was on the driveway, but before I could get in the house to find out why he'd finished early, someone called my name.

"Jill! I'm glad I caught you."

"Monty. I didn't see you there."

"I'm like a ninja, aren't I?"

"Actually, I'm in a bit of a hurry."

"I won't keep you. I wanted to make sure you had my date in your diary. I know what a busy person you are."

"What *date*?"

"The grand opening of Have I Got Internet For You."

"Oh, right, the internet café. When is that again?"

"A week on Wednesday. Charlie Barley is doing the honours."

"He's the carrot guy, right?"

"That's him. Host and star of Where's My Carrot."

"I'll try to make it, but as you said, I am rather busy."

"You won't want to miss this, Jill. It's a once in a lifetime opportunity because Charlie is going to retire at the end of the year. It starts at nine o'clock, and I'm expecting a big crowd."

"Right, okay. Anyway, I have to get going."

"Don't forget to bring a carrot with you."

"Sorry?"

"There's free champers for everyone who turns up with a carrot. That was my idea. Good, eh?"

"Brilliant, yeah. I have to go now."

"Next Wednesday at nine."

"Got it."

Jack was standing in the hallway. "I see Monty collared you too."

"That man is insane."

"Don't forget to take your carrot next week."

"Where does he come up with these crazy ideas? Anyway, how come you're home so early?"

"I had to go and see one of my oppos in Washbridge this afternoon. It wasn't worth driving all the way back to West Chipping afterwards, so I decided to work from home."

"*Work from home*? Is that code for watching TenPin TV?"

"I did get a bit of work done." He grinned. "But, purely coincidentally, there was a re-run of Saturday's top national semi-final clash being shown this afternoon."

"You have the life of Riley."

"By the way, did you spot the graffiti on the bridge?"

"Yeah."

"Any idea who might have done it?"

"None, but it should be gone soon. I found someone to

remove it, and he was working on it when I drove past just now."

"Should we be worried about this?"

"I don't think so. Who takes any notice of graffiti?"

Although I did my best to sound nonchalant for Jack's sake, I was actually rather concerned. It was hard enough living as a sup in the human world without someone trying to broadcast that fact to all and sundry. I would have to hope that it turned out to be an isolated incident.

Chapter 4

For some reason, I couldn't face breakfast.

"Jack, will you be staying home to watch TV again this morning? Sorry I meant to say: *working from home?*"

"You're so funny. No, I'll be in work all day today." He was studying the contents of the cupboard. "We still don't have any muesli."

"That's because you haven't bought any, and don't tell me that you haven't had the time. You could have done it yesterday afternoon before you embarked on your TenPin TVathon."

"What are these granola bars like?"

"I didn't realise we had any."

"They were at the back of the cupboard, behind the box of cake mix that you've never used. Hold on, it doesn't matter, it looks like they were out of date over two months ago."

"I shouldn't worry about that. They make those dates up."

"Are you being serious?" He looked at me like I'd lost my mind. "Those dates are to stop you being poisoned."

"You're so gullible. They're just a way to get you to throw away perfectly good food and buy more. The G & M test is much more accurate."

"What's the G & M test?"

"'G' for has it turned green? 'M' for are there maggots?"

"Gross." He threw the granola bars into the bin. "I'm not going to risk it."

"You're such a wuss."

***

Jack had already left for work, and I'd just seen Mr Ivers drive away, so at least I wouldn't get ambushed by him this morning.

"Buzz! Buzz!" One of the two giant wasps shouted at me.

"Tony?"

"It's Clare, actually. Morning, Jill."

My next-door neighbours were obsessed with cosplay; they went to conventions most weekends.

"Morning, Jill," the other wasp said.

"Hi, Tony. Let me guess — is it InsectCon?"

"Actually, it's BeeCon."

"Oh? Aren't those wasp costumes?"

"See!" Clare turned to her wasp partner. "I told you that people would know."

"Sorry," I said. "Did I say the wrong thing?"

"It's okay, Jill. Tony forgot to order the bee costumes in time, so when we tried to get them, there wasn't one to be had anywhere. Tony said we should hire these instead, and that no one would notice. As if."

"I've already explained," Tony fired back. "I thought you'd ordered the bee costumes."

"I ordered the costumes for DentistCon."

"Sorry, guys." I began to edge towards the car. "I really do have to get going. I have an early meeting."

I don't think they heard me; they were too busy arguing. I had to hope it wouldn't come to stings.

I was pleased to see that the graffiti had gone. Tatts had made a really good job of removing it; there wasn't even the 'shadow' which sometimes gets left behind.

By the time I'd parked the car, I was beginning to feel hungry, and regretted my decision to skip breakfast, so I made a quick diversion down the high street to Coffee Games.

"Morning, Jill." Sarah was on duty again.

"Hi. Can I get a caramel latte to go, please? And give me one of those pain au chocolat, would you?"

Just then, there was an almighty clatter behind me. It seemed to come from one of the booths near the window. Then a similar sound came from the back of the shop.

Sarah appeared to be totally unconcerned that the shop seemed to be collapsing around us.

"What's happening?" I said.

"It's okay. It's Jenga day."

"Oh, right. Have you had many sups in since yesterday?"

"A few more, mostly vampires for some reason." She handed me the coffee and pastry. "Between you and me, vampires give me the creeps."

"Isn't the owner a vampire?"

"Yes, but fortunately, I don't have much to do with him. I can't get past the idea that they think it's okay to drink blood." She shivered at the thought. "Hey, have you seen all the flyers for that clown thing?"

"You mean the Clownathon?"

"Yeah, it looks like fun. I've always loved clowns."

"Right, well I'd better get going. Lots to do."

Freak!

After what Grandma had said the previous day, I decided to walk down to West Street, and take a look at the two bridal shops before they opened. I was curious to see if Grandma really was stealing Kathy's ideas.

Much to my surprise, Kathy was already in the shop, so I knocked on the window.

"It was nice of you to bring me a coffee," she said when she unlocked the door.

"This is mine. I haven't had any breakfast, and besides, I didn't expect you to be here or the shop to be open yet."

"It isn't, but I wanted to change this display before we open."

"Couldn't May have done that?"

"It's her day off."

"Grandma isn't a big fan of May. Or you, for that matter."

"What makes you say that?"

"She was complaining to me yesterday about how you've stolen all of her ideas, and how rude May was to her."

"I know she's your grandmother, Jill, but seriously, that woman is a real piece of work. And as for May being rude to her, that's because I told her I didn't want your grandmother snooping around the shop when I wasn't here."

"I kind of figured that."

"It's your grandmother who rips off every idea I come up with."

"You must be doing something right because you seem to have got her rattled."

"Good, I'm glad." Kathy's gaze locked onto my pastry. "That pain au chocolat looks nice."

"It is."

"It's rather big for one person."

"I wouldn't have said so."

"I have a knife in the back. I could cut it in half to make it more manageable if you like?"

"And pinch half for yourself, I assume?"

"It's kind of you to offer. It'll make up for the coffee you didn't buy me."

After I'd eaten my (smaller) half of the pastry, I made my way back up the high street, and was almost at my office building when my phone rang.

"Jill, It's Hodd. I hope I didn't wake you."

Cheek!

"Actually, I'm on my way into the office."

"Right, only I know you townies like a lie-in."

"Did you manage to arrange for me to visit Myrtle?"

"Yeah, that's why I'm calling. One o'clock this afternoon. Is that okay for you?"

"That's fine."

"Her lawyer, Bill Long, will meet you at the gates at a quarter to."

"Okay, I'll be there. Thanks for calling."

"Men!" Mrs V was red in the face, and clearly unhappy about something.

"Any man in particular?"

"Armi."

"What did he do?"

"He told me off because I put the double-flasher on."

"The *what*?"

"You know: the flashers. Indicators or whatever it is they're called."

"I know what an indicator is, but what's a *double-flasher*?"

"It's when both flashers come on at the same time."

"You mean the hazard warning lights. Why did you put them on?"

"I didn't realise I'd done it. I was trying to turn the heater up, and I must have caught that big red button. It's a stupid place to put it if you ask me."

"Are you and Armi okay now?"

"No, I told him I was going to get someone else to teach me to drive. Someone with a better temperament."

"That's probably for the best. It's never a good idea to have driving lessons with a relative."

"I was thinking that you could teach me."

"Me?"

"That's if you don't mind using your car?"

"My car?"

"We could do it at lunchtimes."

"I'd love to."

"Great."

"Unfortunately, it isn't allowed."

"Why's that?"

"Jack organised the insurance cover for us. He got a special deal which included a stipulation that we weren't allowed to give driving lessons in either of our cars." I edged my way towards my office door. "I'm really sorry."

"I suppose I'll have to look up driving schools, then."

"Sorry again, Mrs V."

"You could lie for England." Winky grinned. "You're quick though, I'll give you that. You came up with that line about the insurance company without even missing a beat."

"I don't like lying to Mrs V, but my nerves aren't up to

giving her driving lessons."

"The old bag lady shouldn't be allowed anywhere near a car; she's much too old to drive."

"Of course she isn't. I'm not the right person to teach her, that's all."

"Have you done anything about the blinds and this floor yet?"

"Not yet. We only talked about it yesterday."

"Crystal said she might pop over later today. It would be nice if I could tell her that the improvements will happen soon."

"I'll get around to it when I have the time, and my finances allow."

"Your finances?" He rolled his one eye. "That'll be never, then."

"Say if you'd like to stump up the money to pay for them yourself. I'm not too proud to accept money from a cat."

"I would but my cashflow isn't great at the moment. I'll tell her that everything is in hand."

"You do that."

Winky's demeanour suddenly changed, and he scurried away under the sofa. Even before the temperature dropped, I knew I was about to be visited by a ghost—the only question was which one?

"Colonel, Priscilla, how nice to see you both."

"Good day, Jill." There was something different about the colonel, but I couldn't quite put my finger on what it was.

"I like what you've done with your hair, Priscilla."

"Thanks. I wasn't sure if the bob would suit me."

"It definitely does."

"What about me, Jill?" the colonel said.

"Sorry?"

"Do you like what I've done with *my* hair?"

"I — err — it — err — "

Priscilla could see that I was struggling. "He's changed the parting from the right to the left."

"Of course. Yes, it suits you."

"It was Cilla's idea. She thought I needed a change."

"You both look — err — "

"Tickety-boo?"

"Exactly."

"This is only a flying visit, Jill," the colonel said. "We wanted to remind you that it's election day today."

"COG? I'd totally forgotten about that. Any idea how you'll fare?"

"It's too close to call. Harry and Larry have run an amazing campaign."

"I'll have my fingers crossed for you."

"We were actually hoping that you'd join us in GT for the final result tonight. It's being broadcast live on TV, and we've decided to hold a joint party with Harry and Larry in Spooky Wooky. The campaign has been run in a good spirit." He laughed. "Spirit? Do you see what I did there?"

"That's very good." I cringed.

"Regardless of who wins, we intend to celebrate a campaign well run. What do you say? Will you join us?"

"I suppose I could pop over for a little while. What time should I come?"

"The result should be in around nine o'clock."

"Okay. I'll be there just before nine."

***

Mrs V had taken a panicked phone call from a Mr Longacre who was desperate to see me straight away. It had something to do with a missing person, but that was as much as I knew. Other than Myrtle Turtle's case, I had nothing much on, so I'd said I would see him.

When he arrived, shortly after eleven, he was accompanied by a woman — they both appeared to be in some distress.

"Mr and Mrs Longacre, I assume?"

"No, I'm Chris Longacre and this is Judy Blythe. My daughter, Susan, and Judy's son, Mark, have been seeing one another for almost two years now. They've both gone missing, and we're hoping you'll be able to find them."

"Mark would never leave without telling me," Judy managed to say, before bursting into tears.

"It's going to be alright." Chris handed her a tissue. "We'll find them."

"Do they live at home with you?"

"No, they moved into a flat together just over six months ago," Chris said. "It's a bit small, but they've got it looking nice."

"Can you talk me through what happened? From the beginning, please."

Judy was still in tears, so Chris told the story. "It was Mark's birthday on Saturday. Susan had organised some kind of surprise for him."

"A party?"

"No, they're not really 'party people'. They both prefer the quiet life, and enjoy each other's company. Susan didn't give any clues as to what the surprise was, but we do know that they came into Washbridge because they'd been at my house in the afternoon, and took a taxi from there."

"Why the taxi? Were they intending to have a drink?"

"No. They're both teetotal. They took the taxi because they don't have a car."

"And that's the last you saw of them?"

"That's right."

"It is only a couple of days. Is it possible that Susan had booked a short break somewhere?"

Judy had finally managed to stem her tears. "The two of them come over to my house for Sunday lunch every week without fail. If they'd planned on going away somewhere, Mark would have told me."

"If you knew them, you'd understand," Chris said. "They're both quiet, responsible young adults who are very close to their families. They would never do anything to cause us this kind of upset."

"I assume you've been to the police?"

"A fat lot of good they are," Chris fumed. "They dismissed us as over-protective parents, but we know our kids. They simply wouldn't do this."

"What about the taxi company that brought them into Washbridge?"

"We've already talked to them. They checked with the driver who confirmed that he dropped Susan and Mark just down the road from here—on the high street. In fact, it was when Judy and I were trying to retrace their steps that we noticed your sign. That's why we called you."

"Can you help us?" There was desperation in Judy's voice.

"Of course, although I don't have a lot to go on. I'll need

you to let me have photos of Mark and Susan. If you check with my receptionist on the way out, she'll give you an email address to send them to."

"Do you think you'll be able to find them?" Chris said.

"I'm sure I will, and don't worry, everything's going to be okay."

If in doubt, always appear confident.

Chapter 5

"Crystal!" Winky practically squealed with excitement when the grey Persian cat jumped in through the window. One day, I really must try to work out how these cats managed to get up here.

She had what I can only describe as a superior look about her, as she glanced around my office with obvious disdain.

"Nice to meet you, Crystal." I felt obliged to be polite for Winky's sake.

She glanced my way for a few seconds, but then, without so much as a purr, went over to join Winky on the sofa.

"I thought you were going to get this place spruced up, Winky?" she said.

"It's all in hand," he assured her. "Jill has already ordered new blinds, and she's getting someone in to treat the floor."

"I'm Jill, by the way," I said. "In case you're interested."

She wasn't. She continued to ignore me, and to interrogate Winky. "What about this sofa? It's disgusting."

"This is going to be replaced too."

I'd never seen Winky fawn over anyone as much as he was doing with Crystal. It was quite pathetic.

"I hope so." She pulled a sour face. "You can't expect me to sit on here for any length of time."

"Of course not, dearest. You can rely on me."

"Good. Now, didn't you say that you were going to take me out for lunch?"

"I did, my precious, follow me."

"Nice to meet you, too, Crystal," I shouted after her, as they disappeared out of the window.

What a nasty piece of work she was. What on earth was Winky thinking?

***

"I'm going to Longdale Prison, Mrs V."

"What have you done this time, Jill? Will I be able to visit you?"

"I haven't done anything. I'm going to see Myrtle Turtle; she's being held there on remand."

"You had me worried there for a moment."

"I'm not sure if I'll get back to the office today. I may go straight home."

"Okay, dear. By the way, I've managed to find a driving instructor."

"That didn't take you long."

"I was lucky. The first few I tried were all booked up, but Miss Dent was able to fit me in straight away. My first lesson is tomorrow."

"Miss *Dent*?"

"Yes, she was very accommodating. She said I could pick a time to suit myself."

"Has she only just started out in business?"

"No, her advert says she's been doing this for over ten years."

"Right? Well, that's great. Best of luck with the lessons. You'll have to let me know how you get on."

Was I wrong to be concerned that Mrs V's driving instructor seemed to have no other clients? There was probably a perfectly reasonable explanation. And as for her name? I was sure that was one of those unfortunate coincidences.

***

Myrtle's solicitor, Bill Long, was waiting for me outside of Longdale Prison, as arranged.

"How is Myrtle?" I said.

"She's fine. Myrtle's a tough old bird. She's very keen to see you, though."

"Lead the way."

After we'd gone through the security checks, we were shown to a private interview room where Myrtle was waiting for us. I was pleased to see that she'd been allowed to wear her own clothes.

"Jill." She came around the table and shook my hand with that firm grip of hers. "Thank you for coming so quickly."

"My pleasure. I'm so sorry you're being kept in here."

"That's partly my own fault. I think the judge would have granted me bail if I hadn't insisted on having my say about the incompetency of the police and the judicial system."

"Shall we sit down, ladies?" Bill suggested.

The solicitor took notes and made the odd comment, but for the most part, he left Myrtle and me to it.

"How much have Hodd and Jobbs told you, Jill?"

"Only the Cliff Notes version. From what I understand, Rob Evans inherited his grandmother's house in Middle Tweaking, and then became something of a nuisance with his parties and loud music. I believe you confronted him about his actions."

"Someone had to. It was getting beyond a joke. Music blaring out at all hours. People wandering the streets, drunk or worse. It simply wasn't on."

"How did he react when you intervened?"

"He didn't like it. I got the distinct impression that he'd never been on the wrong end of any discipline in his life. He was totally selfish and self-absorbed."

"Myrtle, I'm sorry, but I have to ask this — "

"Did I kill him? No, although the thought had crossed my mind. The first I knew about it was when they pulled his body from the river. I assumed he must have been drunk or stoned, and had fallen in, but it turns out that someone had clobbered him."

"Why have they charged you? What kind of evidence do they have?"

"Apparently, they found traces of the man's hair in cracks on the blades of the water-wheel, which suggests that's where he entered the river."

"On your property, you mean?"

"Yes, and they found his footprints in my back garden too."

"I understand that he died from a head wound. Was that inflicted by the water-wheel?"

"Apparently not. He was struck on the head before he fell into the water."

"Do they have the murder weapon?"

"Not as far as I'm aware."

"Had he ever been in your house or garden while you were there?"

"Never."

"I assume you've told the police that?"

"Yes, for what good it did. Did Hodd and Jobbs tell you

that old Charlie Cross has retired?"

"Yes, on health grounds, I understand."

"That's right, although he does seem to have come through the worst of it. If Charlie had still been on the force, I wouldn't be sitting here now. His replacement, Thorne-In-My-Side, seems to care about only one thing: getting a conviction. Innocent or guilty seems to be pretty much irrelevant to her. I was seen arguing with Evans on the day he died, and his death occurred on my property. Case closed, as far as she's concerned."

"That last argument between you and Evans? Where did that take place?"

"In the pub. I was having a quiet drink alone when he came in. He was drunk, high or both, and started to make a general nuisance of himself. He didn't take kindly to my telling him to leave."

"What happened?"

"Nothing much. He just gave me some verbal abuse on his way out. That was the last time I saw Rob Evans."

"From what I understand, the murder happened later that afternoon?"

"That's what they tell me."

"Where were you at the time?"

"After I left the pub, I went for a walk."

"Alone? Didn't anyone see you?"

"Alone yes, and unfortunately no one did. There's some lovely countryside surrounding Middle Tweaking. I find a brisk walk helps to drive away the stresses of the day."

"Do you have any idea who might have murdered him?"

"None. In the short time he was in the village, he'd made a lot of enemies, but I can't believe any of them would have done this."

"Our time is almost up, ladies." Bill Long looked up from his notes.

"Don't worry, Myrtle." I stood up. "We'll get the charges dropped, and have you out of here in no time."

"I knew I could rely on you, Jill. And if you need any help, Hodd and Jobbs have said they're at your disposal."

"Thanks. That might prove useful. Try to keep your chin up."

When I got back to the car and switched on my phone, there were five missed calls from Kathy. She rarely called me during the daytime. For her to have tried so many times, I knew something must be wrong.

"Kathy? What's up?"

"Thank goodness. I didn't think I was going to get hold of you."

"I was in prison. What's the matter?"

"*Prison*? What did you do?"

"I didn't do anything. I was visiting someone on remand. What's wrong?"

"I need a big favour. Is there any way you could pick up Lizzie from school for me? Pete was supposed to do it, but his van has broken down and he's miles from Washbridge."

"Can't you close the shop for a while and go and get her?"

"I would, but I have a customer coming for her final fitting at three o'clock, which is when Lizzie comes out. I wouldn't ask if it wasn't an emergency."

"Okay, but what about Mikey?"

"He has sports after school today. By the time he's

finished, I'll be able to collect him."

"Do you need to let the school know I'll be picking Lizzie up?"

"Yes, I'll do that now. I owe you one, Jill."

"You most certainly do, and don't think that I won't collect."

***

It was some time since I'd visited Lizzie's school. Waiting at the gates were the usual cliques of mothers, and a few fathers, all watching for their offspring to appear through the double doors. A few of them eyed me with suspicion; a stranger in their midst.

From inside the building came the sound of a bell ringing. As a kid, that final bell of the school day had always been music to my ears. It had meant that I could go home and do something I actually found interesting, instead of all the boring and useless lessons I was forced to endure during the day. And yes, Mr Malone (my old maths teacher), it turns out I was right after all—never once have I needed Pythagoras or his stupid theory. Told you so.

"Auntie Jill!" Lizzie threw her arms around me. "I didn't know you were coming to meet me. Where's Daddy?"

"His van has broken down, so your mummy asked me to collect you."

"Can I get sweets?"

"Do your mummy and daddy usually let you have them?"

"Yes, every day."

I wasn't sure if I was being played or not, but I didn't want Lizzie to think I didn't trust her, so we made a detour to the shop that was just around the corner from the school. Inevitably, she chose those sickly, sweet chews that only kids of a certain age enjoy.

"Are those nice?" I asked, as she popped another brightly coloured chew into her mouth.

"These are my most favourites."

"Good."

"Mummy doesn't usually let me have them."

Oh bum. "You didn't mention that when we were in the shop."

"I forgot."

"It might be best not to tell your mummy that you've had them. She might be mad at me."

"Is it our secret, Auntie Jill?"

"Yeah. Our secret."

"I'm good at keeping secrets."

I would have to hope so. Although Kathy had said I didn't need to discuss the ghost thing with Lizzie, I wanted to make sure she was okay. "Your mummy told me that you've been talking about ghosts a lot recently."

"I know you and Mad said I shouldn't talk about them, but there are two more of them in our house now."

"As well as Caroline?"

"Yes. She's still there. The two other ghosts are grown-ups."

"Are they scaring you or misbehaving?"

"No, they're very nice. I don't know their names though."

"When did you first see them?"

"I'm not sure. Not long ago." Lizzie popped the last of

the chews into her mouth. "How can I see them, but Mikey and Mummy and Daddy can't?"

"If I tell you another secret, do you promise that you won't ever tell anyone?"

"Not even Mummy and Daddy?"

"No one, and especially not your mummy and daddy."

"Okay."

"Some people have special powers."

"Like superheroes?"

"Kind of like that, yes. They're called parahumans."

"That's a funny word." She giggled.

"It is, isn't it? It means that they can see ghosts."

"Am I a parrot human, Auntie Jill?"

"Parahuman, yes."

"Are you one, too?"

"Kind of, yes."

"I like being a para—err?"

"Human."

"It's cool, isn't it?"

"It is. Now, let's take you home, and remember, not a word about this. Or the sweets."

***

I made it to Spooky Wooky just before nine o'clock. The place was crammed, and it took me some time to fight my way through the crowd.

I didn't recognise the ghost behind the counter.

"Hi. Where are Harry and Larry?"

"They're over there, by the TV."

"Okay, thanks."

"Would you like something to eat or drink?"

"No, thanks."

I managed to fight my way to the table where Harry, Larry, the colonel and Priscilla were all seated.

"Jill, you made it." The colonel stood up.

"Hi, Jill." Harry and Larry said in unison.

"You've drawn a good crowd. How long until the results come through?"

"Any minute now. Grab a seat." Larry gestured to the vacant chair next to him.

As everyone waited for the final results to be announced, you could have cut the atmosphere with a knife. I couldn't help but be impressed by the camaraderie that the two sides were displaying—something that I'd never witnessed in any election in the human world.

"Here they come now!" Harry pointed to the screen.

I hadn't appreciated that there were in fact several seats up for grabs, so it was another fifteen minutes before the result we were all waiting for came through.

"*Colonel Briggs, Horatio. Seven thousand, three-hundred and twenty-one votes. Wook, Harry. Seven thousand, Five-hundred and thirty votes. As the returning officer for GT Central, I declare that Harry Wook is duly elected to COG.*"

"Well done, Old Man." The colonel was the first to shake Harry's hand.

"Thanks, Colonel. You gave me a good run for my money."

"Well done, Harry," I said. "Commiserations, Colonel."

"No commiserations necessary, Jill. I'll have to push even harder next time."

The celebrations were set to go on late into the night, but I was exhausted, and ready for my bed. After saying my goodbyes, I started to make my way to the door.

"Jill! Yoohoo!"

"Mum? I didn't realise you were here."

"I'm not surprised with the size of this crowd. Alberto and I are over in the corner with your father and Blodwyn. Why don't you come and join us?"

"Thanks, but I only came to see the result. I'm off home now because I'm bushed."

"Okay, but before you go, did you have any joy finding a holiday home for the four of us?"

My mother had asked if she, my father and their respective partners could use our house as a kind of holiday home in the human world. I couldn't imagine anything worse than having to share our house with my parents, so I'd turned her down flat. Instead, I'd promised that I'd try to find them somewhere suitable. Then, I'd promptly forgotten all about it.

"I—err—not yet, but I—"

"It doesn't matter because we've found an agency here in GT that specialises in placing ghosts with ghost-friendly hosts in the human world. We have an appointment to see them tomorrow."

"That's great. Anyway, I'd better get going. Enjoy the rest of your evening."

Chapter 6

Jack still hadn't got around to replenishing his muesli, so he'd had to settle for toast.

"Jack, darling, I need a couple of favours, please."

"What is it this time?"

"What do you mean: *this time*? I hardly ever ask you for a favour, but if it's too much trouble, it doesn't matter." I gave him my disappointed look — that one never failed.

"I didn't say that. What do you want me to do?"

What did I tell you? Snigger.

"Do you have a contact at the council CCTV office? I want to view the footage for Saturday evening."

"Why?"

"A young couple have gone missing. I know when and where they were dropped off, so if I could get a look at the CCTV, I might get a lead on what happened to them."

"I know some people in that office. I'll have a word, but I'm not promising anything."

"I have every faith in you."

"What's the other favour?"

"I need you to get us an invite for dinner at Kathy's."

"Why me? You should ask her yourself. She's your sister."

"If I do it, she'll think I'm up to something."

"And are you? Up to something?"

"I picked Lizzie up from school yesterday because Peter's van had broken down, and Kathy couldn't get away from the shop."

"You didn't mention it last night."

"I forgot. Anyway, do you remember that I told you Lizzie can see ghosts?"

"She has a little ghost friend, doesn't she?"

"Caroline, yeah, but Lizzie reckons another two ghosts have moved into their house, but these are adults."

"Are they causing problems?"

"I don't think so. Lizzie says they're okay, but I'd like to check them out for myself, to make sure there's nothing fishy going on. I thought if we went over there for dinner, you could keep Kathy and Peter occupied while I investigate."

"Isn't it a little presumptuous of us to invite ourselves?"

"That's another reason why I want *you* to call Kathy. With that silver tongue of yours, you'll be able to do it."

"I suppose I could tell her that I'm tired of eating your awful cooking. She'd believe that."

"I resent that remark, but if it means you'll call her, I'll let you off this once."

"If I'm going to do all of this for you, I'll need a favour in return."

"I might have known. What do you want?"

"Can you get me some muesli?"

"Sure, I'll pick some up on my way home."

"I meant right now. I'm getting withdrawal symptoms."

"What about *my* breakfast?"

"Come on, it's only fair. Two favours for one in return."

"Fine! I'll go and get your stupid muesli."

Blackmail, that's what this was. I grumbled to myself all the way to the corner shop.

Little Jack Corner was standing outside the door. "Here, puss! Here, puss!"

"Morning, Jack. Have you lost your cat?"

"Yes, he doesn't usually stay out for more than a few

hours at a stretch, but he's been missing for almost a day now. Anyway, you don't want to hear about my feline-related problems. Come inside."

"Wow, what have you been doing in here? This is all very impressive."

Throughout the store, there were numerous displays of tinned food, stacked in the most elaborate way. I had to weave my way very carefully down the aisles in order not to knock any of them over.

"I've been preparing all week for the annual Corner Shop Stacking Competition. It's the regional heats tomorrow, and I'm hoping to qualify in the 'Most Stacks' and 'Highest Stacks' categories."

"You must certainly be in with a chance."

"I hope so. What brings you out at this hour of the morning, Jill? Have you run out of custard creams?"

"Not this time."

"What can I get you, then?"

"You may find this surprising, but I actually want a box of muesli. Be honest, Jack, I bet you don't get many people asking for that, do you?"

"It's actually our best-selling breakfast cereal."

I laughed. "Very funny."

"It's true, Jill. The people of Smallwash are very health conscious when it comes to breakfast, but to be honest, I wouldn't have had you down as a muesli eater."

"Me? I'm all about healthy eating. I can't get enough of the stuff."

"Which brand do you prefer?"

"Oh, you know, the usual one."

"We have six different ones, and they're all very popular. Come and see."

I followed him to the breakfast cereal aisle, being careful not to catch any of the elaborate displays en route.

"That one." I pointed to the box I recognised as Jack's favourite brand of sawdust. "And while I'm here, I suppose I might as well stock up on biscuits."

"Ginger nuts? Digestives?"

"Very funny. I'll take the usual. Two packets, please. Wait, better make that three."

I managed to negotiate my way out of the shop, without knocking over a single display. Sitting outside, right next to the door, was an enormous black cat.

"Come here, Boy. Little Jack has been worried about you." I picked him up, opened the door and dropped him inside. "Your cat's here, Jack."

"Ginger? Oh, thank goodness."

Ginger?

Jack came rushing down the aisle, but then stopped dead in his tracks when he saw the black cat. "That's not Ginger!"

Spooked by the sight of Little Jack running towards him, the cat set off down the aisle in the opposite direction.

"I'll be off then." I hurried outside and closed the door behind me. As I walked away, the sound of a thousand tin cans crashing to the floor echoed in my ears.

***

When I arrived in Washbridge, I was still feeling a little guilty about the part I'd played in the destruction of Little Jack's elaborate displays, but how was I supposed to know his cat was ginger?

As I approached my office building, I spotted a woman loitering outside; she looked lost and confused.

"Can I help you?"

"I'm looking for the offices of Jill Maxwell, but I can't seem to find them. This is supposed to be the address, but the sign says Jill and Max Well."

"Don't worry about the sign. You're in the right place. I'm Jill Maxwell. Am I expecting you?"

"I'm actually here for Annabel Versailles."

"She's my PA."

"I'm Maxine, but everyone calls me Maxi. Maxi Dent."

"Miss Dent! You're Mrs V's driving instructor."

"That's right. I'm here to collect Annabel for her first lesson."

"Great." I pointed to the door. "After you."

She reached out to grab the handle, but it seemed to elude her.

"Are you okay, Maxi?"

"Yes, it's these new contact lenses. Ah, there it is." She turned the handle and opened the door.

"Our offices are up the stairs, on the right."

After several attempts, she finally managed to locate the handrail, and then made her way slowly upstairs.

"This door?"

"No, that's a cupboard. It's to your right. Here, allow me."

"Morning, Jill," Mrs V greeted me.

"Morning. Your driving instructor is here. Come in, Maxi."

"I'm really nervous," Mrs V said.

"There's nothing to worry about, Annabel." Maxi was

obviously trying to reassure Mrs V, but for some reason, she appeared to be talking to the filing cabinet. "I'll have you through your test in no time."

"Are you sure you want to do this, Mrs V?" I said.

"Absolutely. I'll show Armi that I'm as good a driver as any man. Come on, Maxi, let's hit the road." Mrs V came around the desk and made for the door.

"This way." I took Maxi by the shoulders and pointed her in the right direction. "Be careful out there, you two."

Oh boy. I hoped Mrs V would get through her first driving lesson unscathed, but I couldn't help but think that her driving instructor was a *Maxi Dent* waiting to happen.

What? Come on, you know you love them.

And then there was Winky.

"What do you think you're doing!" I yelled at him.

"Shush! I need to concentrate. This part is very intricate."

Not a cat to let the grass grow under his paws, Winky had already moved into the tattoo artist business. His client, a thuggish looking cat, was lying on the sofa while Winky worked on his masterpiece.

"Yeah, shut it, lady!" The thug scowled at me. "I don't want my tatt ruined."

"Winky, do you think I could have a quick word, please?"

"Sorry, Bruiser. I'll only be a few minutes."

I led the way to the outer office, so we could have some privacy. "What do you think you're playing at in there?"

"I'm not *playing* at anything. What you witnessed in there is art in its purest form."

"Do you even know how to do a tattoo?"

"Of course I do. I found dozens of how-to videos online."

"That's alright, then. For a moment there, I thought you were winging it. Seriously, do you really think watching a few videos qualifies you to do work on a live subject?"

"You worry too much. Are we done here? Bruiser doesn't like to be kept waiting."

"He looks like a thug to me."

"Shush, don't let him hear you. He's had his problems, but he's done his time, and that's all in the past now."

"What kind of *problems*?"

"Winky!" The thunderous voice came from my office. "What are you doing out there? I don't have all day, you know."

"I have to go." Winky scurried back to his client. "Don't disturb us again."

Did Winky seriously expect me to wait outside my own office while he tattooed some ne'er-do-well? I love that word—I should use it more often. If he did, he was in for a rude awakening because I was going to throw that thug out on his fat backside.

But, before I could do that, my phone rang.

"It's Jack. I've managed to swing it for you to watch the town centre CCTV from last Saturday, but you'll have to get around there straight away because the guy I spoke to goes off shift in an hour."

"Okay. Who do I ask for?"

"Dave de Rave."

"What kind of name is that?"

"That's what he said. I think his parents must be French

or something."

"Okay, thanks. I'll go straight over there. See you later."

"Hold on a second. That's not all. I also spoke to Kathy, and she said they'd be delighted to have us over for dinner tonight."

"Well done, you. Did it take much doing?"

"No, I told her that I was tired of your cooking, and she understood straight away."

Cheek!

Bruiser had been handed a temporary reprieve, but he'd better be gone by the time I got back or there'd be big trouble.

The council offices that monitored the city centre CCTV were only a five minute walk from my building.

"I'm here to see Dave de Rave," I said, in my best French accent. I'm Jill Maxwell—he's expecting me."

The young woman behind the desk blew and then popped a bubble-gum bubble. "Who did you say you wanted to see?"

"Dave de Rave."

"There's no one here of that name."

"He works in the department that monitors the city centre CCTV."

"Oh!" She grinned. "You mean Dave the Rave."

"Do I?"

"Yeah. His name's actually David Edwards, but everyone calls him Dave the Rave."

"Right, well, if you could let him know I'm here, please."

"Sure. Take a seat over there, would you?"

As the receptionist picked up the phone, she made the

fatal mistake of blowing another bubble. It took her several minutes to pull all the gum off the handset before she was able to complete the call. Eventually, though, the man was summoned to reception.

"Jill? I'm Dave the Rave."

The reason for his nickname was now apparent. With his smiley-face t-shirt and baseball cap, the man was a throwback to the nineties rave culture. What surprised me most, though, was the glowstick he was holding.

"Pleased to meet you, Dave." I shook his free hand. "Are you allowed to bring those into work?"

"The glowstick?" He laughed. "It's actually a pen. Realistic, though, isn't it? The missus got it for my birthday."

"I take it you're into nineties music?"

"Best decade ever. I was at Uni in Manchester back then. Good times."

"Did Jack tell you what I wanted to view?"

"He did. I've got it all set up for you. Follow me."

Dave did a quick run-through of the controls, but then left me to it. I had the photos of Mark and Susan on my phone, and I knew approximately when and where the taxi driver had dropped them on the high street, so I was hopeful that it wouldn't take long for me to pick them out.

Three minutes into the footage, the pair appeared — getting out of the taxi. They then walked arm in arm up the high street before disappearing out of range of that camera. After switching to the next camera, I picked up their progress as they took a right off the high street, and walked along the road where my offices are based.

What happened next took me completely by surprise:

when they reached my office building, they went inside.

Chapter 7

Unless Mark and Susan had left by the rear fire exit, their only way out of the building would have been through the same door they went in. I whizzed through several hours of CCTV footage, but there was no sign of them leaving. I was on the point of calling it quits when I saw two young people emerge from the front door.

It wasn't Mark and Susan; it was Lucas and Wendy from Escape, and it was obvious that they were arguing about something.

"How are you doing?" Dave the Rave came back into the room. "Did you find what you were looking for?"

"Not exactly, but it's been very helpful all the same." I stood up. "Thanks for letting me do this."

"No problem." He handed me a note.

"What's this?"

"Do yourself a favour and listen to some good music. These are my favourite nineties playlists on Spotify."

"Err—thanks." I didn't have the heart to tell him that the closest thing I had to Spotify was my vinyl collection.

***

After leaving Dave the Rave, I headed straight back to my building, but instead of going into the office, I walked down the corridor to Escape.

Wendy was on the reception desk; she greeted me with her usual scowl. "Can I help you?"

"Is Lucas in?"

"He's in the office."

"I'd like to speak to you both, please."

"Is it important? He's doing the accounts."

"It's extremely important. So, if you wouldn't mind."

She made a big show of sighing, but went to get Lucas, anyway.

"Hi, Jill." Lucas at least managed a half-smile. "What can I do for you?"

"When I bumped into you two on Monday, you were about to tell me there'd been some kind of problem. Would you like to tell me what's wrong?"

"Nothing's wrong," Wendy said. "Everything's fine."

Despite Wendy's words, I could tell by Lucas' reaction that things were anything but fine. I took out my phone, brought up the photo of Mark and Susan, and held it out for them to see. "Are you sure there's nothing you'd like to tell me?"

"We don't know what's happened—" Lucas began.

"Be quiet, Lucas." Wendy closed him down. "This has nothing to do with her."

"I think you'll find it has everything to do with me. The parents of these two young people have hired me to find them. I've been watching CCTV footage from Saturday night. I saw this couple come into the building, but there's no sign of them leaving again."

"The CCTV must be faulty," Wendy said. "You can't rely on—"

"Stop it, Wendy!" Lucas interrupted her. "We have to tell Jill."

"Tell me what?"

"Come on through to the office." Lucas led the way. Wendy was about to follow us when he held up his hand. "You'd better stay on reception in case there are any customers."

She didn't look happy, but she didn't argue.

"What's going on, Lucas?" I said, once we were in his office.

"The couple in the photograph are stuck somewhere in the escape room."

"What do you mean *stuck*? Can't you let them out?"

"I wish we could. We don't know where they are or how to find them."

"But it's your escape room."

"I know." He shook his head.

"I think you'd better tell me exactly what's going on here."

"We wanted to provide the ultimate escape room experience. The problem with other escape rooms is that there are a limited number of rooms and puzzles. We wanted something different."

"So you used magic?"

"That's right."

"If you've cast a spell, why don't you reverse it?"

"I wish it was that easy."

"Why isn't it?"

"The escape room isn't powered by *our* magic. It's powered by a 'world generator' spell."

"I've read about those at CASS. They were never intended to be used for something like an escape room. Where did you get it from?"

"We bought it from a wizard called Columbus Dark."

"Why don't you get him to sort it out, then?"

"We've tried. As soon as we realised the young couple were trapped, we tried to contact him, but we can't get hold of him."

"Well that's just dandy, isn't it?"

"I'm really sorry."

"You can't be all that sorry because, as far as I can tell, you're still open for business."

"I wanted to close but—" His words trailed off.

"But Wendy insisted you remain open?"

He nodded.

"Okay, I'll tell you what's going to happen. As soon as I leave, you're going to put the 'Closed' sign up. And if Wendy objects, tell her to come and see me. In the meantime, I'll see if I can find this Dark guy."

"You're a really powerful witch, Jill. Couldn't you use your magic to get the young couple out of there?"

"From what little I've read about world generators. They're not single spells that can simply be reversed. They're comprised of a suite of interlaced spells. By the time I've worked out how they all interact, it would have been quicker to track down Dark."

"Okay. I really do appreciate your helping us like this."

"Just make sure you shut up shop as soon as I leave."

"I will. I promise."

Mrs V was back from her driving lesson, and as far as I could tell, she'd come through the experience unscathed.

"Did the driving lesson go okay, Mrs V?"

"It was excellent. Maxi is a fantastic instructor."

"That's good to know. I must admit, I was a little worried."

"You're referring to her eyesight, I assume?"

"Yeah."

"I was worried too when she asked me to guide her to the car, but when we got there, she removed her contact lenses and put on her regular glasses. She was fine after that. I think she's decided to abandon the contacts."

"Probably for the best. The lesson itself went okay, then?"

"Absolutely. Maxi said she didn't think I'd need more than eighty lessons."

"Eighty?"

"Apparently, it's one for each year of your age plus ten percent."

"How many are you planning on having each week?"

"Only the one, dear. They are rather expensive."

"Right, so that's about a year and a half, then?"

"You can't rush these things. Better safe than sorry."

"That's true."

When I went through to my office, I was relieved to find that Bruiser had already taken his leave.

"About time too." Winky jumped off the sofa. "I'm starving. Tattooing is hungry work."

"How did the tattoo turn out?"

"Excellent, even if I do say so myself."

"Was Bruiser pleased with it?"

"He was delighted. He's going to recommend me to all of his friends."

"I'm not sure that's a good thing."

"Of course it is. The money I earn from these tattoos will pay for new blinds, a new sofa, and treating the floor."

"*You're* going to pay for them?"

"What choice do I have? By the time you can afford to pay, Crystal will have already dumped me."

***

Jack and I were getting ready to go over to Kathy and Peter's place for dinner.

"Don't forget," I said while struggling with the zip on my dress. "As soon as we've finished dinner, we're coming home."

"You really are unbelievable. First, you get me to wangle us an invite to dinner, and now you're planning how quickly we can get away afterwards."

"You know why I want to go over there. I need to check that those new ghosts aren't misbehaving."

"I realise that, but there's no reason why we can't have a chat with Peter and Kathy while we're there."

"About what?"

"I don't know. Anything."

"But you know what Kathy's like. She'll only bore the pants off us, discussing the bridal shop."

"Not necessarily. We could always lead the conversation."

"If you think I'm going to spend all evening listening to you and Peter discussing the finer points of ten-pin bowling, you've got another think coming."

"What are you planning to do about the ghosts, anyway?" He laughed. "I can't believe I said that sentence out loud."

"I'll have to play it by ear. By rights, ghosts should only haunt a location where they once lived, or where they have some other strong connection. The first thing I'm going to ask them is what connection, if any, they have with Kathy's house. If they don't have a good reason for being there, I'll politely suggest they return to Ghost

Town."

"*Politely?*"

"I'm always polite; you know that."

***

"Welcome to chez Brooks." Kathy greeted us at the door.

"Thanks for inviting us."

"I was under the impression that you'd invited yourselves." She laughed. "Pete is taking the kids to his mother's house for a few hours, so the grown-ups can have an intelligent conversation. Oh, and you can join in too if you like, Jill."

"Ha ha." My sister, the comedian.

Just then, Peter arrived home.

"Hi, you two. Why haven't you offered them a drink, Kathy?"

"Give me a chance — they've only just walked through the door. Dinner is going to be another twenty minutes, so you may as well all go through to the lounge."

"Can I help with anything?" I offered.

"It's okay. I've got it covered."

This was working out better than I could have hoped. Kathy was busy in the kitchen, so if I could get Jack to distract Peter, I'd be able to go on my ghost hunt.

"Jack, didn't you say you wanted to challenge Peter to a rematch?"

"Sorry?" He looked puzzled.

"You remember." I winked at him. "Ten-pin bowling. You said you were going to ask if he wanted a rematch."

"Oh yeah, that's right." The penny had finally dropped.

"I know you must be feeling deflated by the way I thrashed you last time, buddy, but I thought it only fair to give you a chance to get your own back."

"*Thrashed?*" Peter scoffed. "As I recall it, you squeaked a win on the last frame."

Bingo! While they debated whether the first match had been a whitewash or a close-run thing, I slipped out of the room and crept upstairs.

It didn't take long for me to track down the ghosts. As soon as I walked into the main bedroom, the temperature dropped dramatically. No wonder Kathy had thought the heating was on the blink.

Two ghosts, a young man and woman, were sitting on the bed, chatting. They hadn't noticed me walk into the room, so I cleared my throat to get their attention. "Hello, there."

"You can see us!" The man seemed genuinely surprised.

"I can."

"Do you live here too?"

"No, this is my sister's house. I'm just visiting."

"Your sister can't see us. None of them can except for the little girl."

"That's my niece, Lizzie. She's a parahuman. What I don't understand is why you've decided to move in here."

"We were told that the people who lived here were expecting us."

"Who told you that?"

"The company who sold us this package."

"I'm sorry, but you've totally lost me now. Would you like to start at the beginning and explain how come you're here?"

"I'm Henry, and this is my fiancée, Jacqueline."

"Nice to meet you both. I'm Jill."

"We've been looking for somewhere to stay in the human world for some time now, but because we have no living relatives, it hasn't been possible. Then we saw the advertisement for Ghost Horizons. Have you heard of them?"

"I can't say I have. What do they do?"

"They find ghost-friendly hosts, in the human world, who are happy to have ghosts move in with them."

"So, you're saying that Ghost Horizons put you onto this house?"

"That's right. The whole point is that the hosts are supposed to have agreed to the hauntings, but that doesn't appear to be the case here. Your sister, her husband and the little boy seem oblivious to our presence. Even though the little girl can see us, she obviously wasn't expecting us. To tell you the truth, we're beginning to think we've been conned. The last thing we want to do is intrude upon some unsuspecting humans."

"I think you're right. It sounds to me like Ghost Horizons have taken your money under false pretences."

"I feel like such a fool."

"I wouldn't be so hard on yourself. Ghost Horizons appear to be the ones at fault here."

"There's nothing else for it. We may as well go back to GT, and see if we can get our money back. I'm sorry for any inconvenience we may have caused."

"No problem. I hope you manage to get a refund."

With that, the two ghosts took their leave.

"Jill." Kathy walked into the bedroom. "Who were you talking to?"

"I wasn't."

"I heard you say something about a refund."

"I—err—it's these shoes. They're cutting into my heels. I was just saying I'd have to take them back for a refund."

"You said that to yourself?"

"I sometimes don't realise I'm talking out loud."

"Right. Anyway, why are you in our bedroom?"

"I—err—took a wrong turn. Is dinner ready?"

"Yes, I've been calling you for the last two minutes. Come on down or it'll be cold." She started for the door, but then hesitated. "That's strange."

"What is?"

"It's been freezing in this room for some time now. Don't you remember I told you that I thought the central heating was on the blink? It seems to be working again. It's the warmest it's been in here for ages."

"Call off the search party—I've found her," Kathy said when we joined the guys in the dining room. "She reckons she'd taken a wrong turn, but I think she was checking out the new wallpaper in our bedroom."

"You got me. I love what you've done with that flock."

"Anyway, I'm glad you and Jack have come over. I've got so many things to tell you about my plans for the bridal shop."

Sigh.

Chapter 8

"What do you make of what the ghosts told you?" Jack asked over breakfast the next morning.

"It sounds to me like someone in GT is running a con, and I'm worried that my mother and father may be about to fall for it."

"How come?"

"I didn't tell you this, but they asked if we'd mind if they moved in with us."

"You're joking."

"I wish I was. They seriously thought we'd welcome them with open arms."

"I know they're your parents, but I'm not sure I'd want to share the house with ghosts."

"Don't worry. I told them it was never going to happen, but when I saw my mother on election night, she said they'd made other arrangements. She mentioned a company that was going to set them up with a suitable house here in the human world."

"And you think it might be the same company that sent those ghosts to live at Kathy's?"

"I'd bet my life on it."

"What do you plan on doing?"

"I'm going to nip over to GT this morning. Hopefully, I'll catch her before she's handed over any money."

***

Even though I now knew where Mark and Susan were (well kind of), it wasn't something I could share with their worried parents. Can you imagine how that particular conversation would go?

"*Hi, it's Jill. I have some good news. I know where your kids are.*"

"*Thank goodness. Where are they? Are they okay?*"

"*I think so. They're trapped in a world generator.*"

"*Right? What's one of those?*"

"*It's a magic spell, or more accurately, a suite of interlaced spells.*"

"*Magic?*"

"*I know what you're thinking, but go with me on this one.*"

"*Can you get them back?*"

"*Yes, maybe, I'm not sure. The thing is that this particular world generator seems to have malfunctioned.*"

"*Can you repair it?*"

"*I can't, but I know a man who can. Maybe.*"

"*Great. When can he do it?*"

"*There's a slight problem: No one knows where he is.*"

See what I mean? I came to the conclusion that there was nothing to be gained from contacting my clients until I had something a little more concrete to tell them.

From what I'd read at CASS, I knew that there were very few wizards who were capable of creating a world generator. Someone must know where I could find Columbus Dark—maybe Grandma could give me some suggestions as to where to start my enquiries.

Her phone rang out for the longest time, and I was beginning to think that she wasn't going to answer when:

"What is it?"

"Grandma? Are you okay. You sound—"

"Half asleep? That's because I *was* asleep until you woke me."

"Sorry, I thought you were an early riser."

"I am, but not on my day off. Do you actually want something or did you just call to disturb my beauty sleep?"

"I have a quick question for you, that's all."

"What are you waiting for, then? Get on with it!"

"I need to find a wizard called Columbus Dark. He has built a—"

"Columbus? What do you want with him?"

"Do you know him?"

"I would hope so. He and I were together for a while. Before your grandfather and I met, obviously."

"I had no idea."

"Why are you looking for him?"

"He sold a world generator to a wizard and witch, who are running an escape room next door to my offices."

"What's an *escape room* when it's at home?"

"People, humans mainly, pay to get locked in a room. Then they have to solve puzzles in order to escape."

"They pay to be locked in a room, you say?"

"Yeah, and it can be quite expensive."

"The more I learn about humans, the more I despair."

"Are you still in touch with him? Columbus Dark?"

"I haven't seen him for years. Decades, in fact."

"That's a shame."

"That doesn't mean I don't know where he's likely to be. You should try the Sinkhole Tavern. He used to spend most of his time in there, and if I know Columbus, he probably still does."

"That's great. Where is the—?"

Too late—she'd gone.

I considered calling her back, but decided not to push my luck. It surely wouldn't be too difficult to locate the tavern she'd mentioned.

***

Before I could go in search of Columbus Dark, I had an appointment with Charlie Cross, the retired sergeant, in West Chipping. But first, I had to try to stop my parents handing over their money to the fraudsters, Ghost Horizons.

"Jill? What are you doing here?" My mother was clearly surprised to see me standing there. "Are you okay?"

"I'm fine. Can I come in for a minute?"

"Of course. Would you like a cup of tea?"

"Not for me, thanks. Where's Alberto?"

"He's out the back. He likes to wipe the dew off the gnomes first thing in the mornings."

"Right. I wanted a quick word about this holiday home idea of yours."

"If you're feeling guilty because you turned us down, there's no need. I never should have asked."

"No, it's not that. What's the name of the company that is arranging the holiday home for you in the human world?"

"Ghost Horizons. Why?"

"Have you paid them any money yet?"

"No, we're supposed to go into their offices tomorrow to pay them. We'll have to go to the bank first to draw out the cash because they don't accept any other form of payment."

"I bet they don't."

"Is there some kind of problem with them? What have you heard?"

I told her about the ghosts who had been sent by Ghost Horizons to live at Kathy's house.

"Are you trying to tell me that these charlatans aren't vetting the hosts at all?"

"That's exactly what I'm telling you. Once you've handed over the money, you could end up just about anywhere."

"That's outrageous. The whole point of paying for the service was so we could live in a house where the hosts welcomed us with open arms. Wait until I see them; I'll give them a piece of my mind. And I imagine your father will have plenty to say to them too."

"You mustn't do that."

"Why not? They almost cheated us out of a good part of our savings."

"That may make you feel better, but they'll still be able to cheat other ghosts out of their money."

"What do you suggest I do, then?"

"Why don't you have a word with Constance Bowler at GT police station? I'm sure she'd be interested in setting up some kind of sting operation to catch these people red-handed. We need to put them out of business once and for all. She'll probably need you to help, though. That's if you're up for it?"

"Sign me up. No one tries to steal my hard-earned cash and gets away with it."

***

My first visit to Middle Tweaking, some time ago now, had been to take part in a murder mystery evening held at the local pub: The Old Trout. Kathy had dragged me there, and if I recall correctly, I'd been the only one to pick out the 'murderer'.

What's that you say? It was Jack who picked out the murderer? That can't possibly be right.

Anyway, moving on. Not long after that evening, there had been a real-life murder in the village. Madge Hick, the postmistress, had been murdered by the then landlord of the Old Trout, Trevor Total. That was the first time I'd worked alongside Myrtle, and she'd left an indelible impression on me. If nothing else, it had dispelled any misconceptions I'd harboured that age might be a barrier to effectiveness. She was as sharp as a razor, and as tough as old boots. During that investigation, Myrtle had introduced me to Charlie Cross, who was a sergeant in the police force at the time. Now retired, on health grounds, he'd agreed to meet with me, to discuss the recent murder of Robert Evans.

"Jill, how very nice to see you again." Charlie greeted me at the door of his cottage, which was located half a mile outside the village of Middle Tweaking. He'd lost a little weight since the last time I'd seen him, but otherwise, he seemed in rude health.

"Lovely place you have here, Charlie."

"Thank you. I've just put on the kettle. Would you like tea?"

"That would be lovely."

While he was in the kitchen, I took a look around the lounge. On the walls were several photographs of Charlie in uniform, from early pictures of a fresh-faced constable, to more recent shots of him taken in the village. Conspicuous by their absence were any photographs of family.

"There you go, Jill." He handed me the cup. "Milk and one and two-thirds sugar. I hope that's right?"

"How on earth did you know?"

"I have my spies." He laughed.

"How long were you in the force, Charlie?"

"All my working life—man and boy. I never rose above sergeant, but that suited me down to the ground. I'd no desire to move into management; there was enough paperwork at my level. If I remember correctly, your young man is in the force, isn't he?"

"Jack is actually my husband now. We married quite recently."

"Congratulations."

"Thanks, and yes, he's a detective based in West Chipping. Are you—err—were you married, Charlie?"

"Me? No. There was someone once, but things didn't work out."

I didn't ask him, but I couldn't help but wonder if that *someone* had been Myrtle. She'd told me that they'd once been an item.

When we'd finished our tea, we got down to business.

"I imagine Myrtle has told you about Robert Evans?" Charlie wore a pained expression as he spoke the man's name.

"I understand he inherited his grandmother's house here in the village."

"That's right. Josie Plumb was a wonderful lady, and a leading light on the allotments committee. How she ever ended up with a grandson like Robert is beyond me. There were wild parties, loud music, drink and goodness knows what else. If I'd still been on the force, I would have shut it down."

"Didn't your successor have anything to say about all these goings on?"

"You mean Thorne? She wouldn't lower herself to get involved with anything so trivial. She should never have been assigned to the area because she doesn't understand village life at all. She was quick enough to get involved with the murder, though."

"I take it you don't rate her?"

"I do not, but I wouldn't want you to think it's because she's a woman or because she's young. That makes no difference in my book. Take you — you're a young woman but from what I hear from Myrtle, you could run rings around almost anyone."

"Myrtle told me that they haven't found the murder weapon?"

"That's right, and I think that's going to be the key to solving this case. The other evidence is mostly circumstantial, but it's all stacked against Myrtle. There are any number of witnesses who saw her arguing with Evans, and it's common knowledge there was no love lost between them. But it's the evidence they found on Myrtle's property that could end up convicting her."

"The footprints in the garden, you mean?"

"That and the hair that was stuck in the water-wheel."

"Myrtle insists that Evans was never on her property while she was there."

"I believe her, but there's no getting away from the fact that he was in her garden at some point, and that he entered the river close by the waterwheel. The thing you have to remember, Jill, is that there's no easy access to that back garden, other than through the house."

"Are you saying you think that Robert Evans was

actually inside Myrtle's house?"

"I can't be sure, but it's difficult to see how he could have got into the back garden any other way. There's a huge wall around it, with razor wire on the top."

"*Razor wire?*"

"Myrtle took her security very seriously."

"So it would seem. If he didn't scale the wall, and Myrtle didn't let him into the house, then how did he get into the garden?"

"If you can work that out, Jill, you'll be a lot closer to knowing what really happened that day."

"Apart from Myrtle, who had access to her house?"

"Hodd and Jobbs, obviously. No one else I can think of." Charlie drank the last of his tea. "There was the cleaner, I suppose."

"Myrtle has a cleaner?"

"Not now, but some time back, Myrtle injured her ankle and was laid up for several weeks, so she brought in a cleaner to help around the place. Once Myrtle was back on her feet, she let her go."

"The cleaner, was she a local? Do you know her name?"

"She doesn't live in the village. Hodd and Jobbs will probably be able to give you her details."

We kicked the thing around for another half hour or so, but it was obvious that Charlie was as baffled as everyone else as to who had murdered Robert Evans.

"Thanks for your time, Charlie."

"My pleasure. I may be retired, but that doesn't mean I've been put out to pasture yet. If there's anything you need—anything at all, give me a shout."

Chapter 9

My phone rang, and I could see from the caller ID that it was Chris Longacre, Susan's father.

"Jill, we just wondered if you had any news for us?"

"Nothing concrete yet, I'm afraid."

"Oh." There was so much disappointment contained in that one tiny word.

"I am following up a lead, though."

"Really? What's that?"

"A possible sighting of Mark and Susan."

"Where?"

"In the city centre."

"That's something, isn't it?"

"It might be, but I wouldn't want you to get your hopes up yet."

"What's the next step?"

"I'm trying to track down someone who may have more information on their whereabouts."

"Who's that?"

Oh boy, this conversation wasn't going well.

"Chris, I'm sorry, but I have an urgent call on the other line. I promise I'll let you know as soon as I have anything to report."

"But, Jill, is—?"

I ended the call, and then ignored his repeated attempts to phone me back. I felt terrible leaving them hanging like that—they must be going through hell—but what could I do? There was nothing else I could tell them. At least, nothing that wouldn't make me look like some kind of crazy woman.

***

"Is that anti-jamming thingy still working, Jill?" Mrs V said.

"Sorry?"

"That device you had installed some time ago. Is it still operational?"

It suddenly all came flooding back to me. Many moons ago, Mrs V had been convinced that someone was interfering with her knitting, by installing electronic devices in our offices. That was, of course, total nonsense, but the only way I could put her mind at ease was by telling her that I'd had an anti-jamming device installed (whatever one of those was).

"Err—yeah, it's still working. Why do you ask?"

"That despicable crochet crowd have organised their annual conference on the same day as our knitting conference. I didn't think I'd see the day when they'd stoop so low."

"But don't you crochet as well as knit?"

"Shush!" She glanced around nervously. "You don't know who might be listening."

"They can't listen in. Not now we have the anti-jamming device."

"Of course. Sorry, Jill. This whole incident has set my nerves on edge."

"Why don't you have a joint conference: Knitters and Crocheters?"

She looked aghast. "Don't be ridiculous. That would never work."

"Sorry—it was a silly suggestion. What exactly is it you're worried about them overhearing?"

"Those crocheters will employ every dirty trick in the book. I don't want to risk them stealing any of our ideas."

"I see. Well, you can rest assured this office is totally secure."

When I went through to my office, Winky was sitting on the window sill. "The man is coming in later today, to measure these."

"Measure what?" I had no clue what he was talking about.

"The windows of course. For the new blinds, which I'm paying for out of the goodness of my heart. I hope you appreciate it."

"Of course I do. I'd prefer grey if it's all the same to you."

"Grey is much too boring. I was thinking purple."

"I'm not having purple blinds in here."

"Okay, okay. No purple."

"I mean it, Winky. I hate purple."

"Message received and understood."

***

Mid-afternoon, I had an unexpected visit from Daze.

"I thought I should check if you were aware of the graffiti, Jill."

"I am, but it's okay. I've had it removed from the bridge."

"Which bridge?"

"The toll bridge near Smallwash. Isn't that what you were talking about?"

"No, I meant the graffiti on the building behind the old

sock factory, and there's some more around the back of the swimming baths."

"What does it say?"

"Jill is a Witch. What did the graffiti on the toll bridge say?"

"The same thing. Don't worry, I'll get those others removed too."

"There's no need. I've already got Laze on it."

"Thanks, I appreciate that."

"Do you have any idea who might be behind it?"

"No, but when I find out, they'll wish they'd never been born."

"There's something else I wanted to discuss with you; something much more serious. Do you remember the blood distribution network?"

"Of course. The last I heard, Blaze said he thought you were getting close to Mr Big, and he was hoping to close the network down soon."

"We did manage to arrest Mr Big, but it seems that there were any number of Mr Not-so-Bigs queuing up to take his place."

"Does that mean the network is still operating?"

"Yes, but it's even worse than that. The original Mr Big did at least have some kind of quality control for the blood that he was peddling. Whoever has taken over doesn't seem to care what damage he does. Several vampires have died from drinking contaminated blood already."

"That's terrible. What are you doing about it?"

"The only thing we can do is get the word out to as many people as possible. That's not easy because most of the shops who are in the network are operating under the radar, so there's no way of knowing if we've covered them all. In the meantime, we're expecting more fatalities. If you know of any shops owned or run by vampires, who you suspect might be dealing blood, please pass on this information."

"Of course."

"Thanks. It's a particularly horrible way to go. After drinking the contaminated blood, the vampire breaks out in green boils, and is dead within a few hours."

"I never cease to be amazed by the depths some people will stoop to just to make a few pounds."

***

Not long after Daze had left, it suddenly occurred to me that Coffee Games could be a target for the blood distribution network. I'd never seen anyone buying blood in there, but it wouldn't do any harm for me to have a quiet word with Sarah, the new assistant.

"The usual, Jill?" She seemed to have grown into her new job.

"No, thanks. I wanted a quick word in private if that's possible."

"Oh? Okay, but I can't be away from the counter for long."

"It'll only take a minute, I promise."

After getting one of the other staff to cover for her, she joined me at a quiet table near the back of the shop.

"I need to ask you a question, and it's important that you're completely honest with me."

"Right?"

"Do you sell human blood in here?"

"What? Of course not."

"Are you absolutely positive about that?"

"Yes. What's this all about, Jill?"

"There's a criminal gang who are selling human blood through small high street shops such as this one. They usually target shops that are run or managed by vampires, and in particular coffee shops."

"I had no idea that anything like this was happening in the human world, but I can promise you there's nothing like that going on in here."

"That's good to hear because I've just been told that there's a bad batch of blood in circulation; it's already killed a number of vampires."

"That's awful."

I handed her my card. "If you see or hear anything suspicious, please call me straight away."

"I will. I promise."

***

As I walked back up the high street, someone shouted, "Cooee!"

"Deli, I didn't see you there." If I had, I would have turned around and walked in the opposite direction.

"Have you heard from Madeline, Jill?"

"Not since the wedding. Haven't you?"

"Not a word. That girl has always been the same. She doesn't realise how much I worry about her."

"I'm sure she's fine. Mad can look after herself."

"I suppose so. Anyway, I wanted to let you know about my new business venture."

"Are you giving up the nail bar?"

"No, don't be silly. That place is a little goldmine. We've started to offer a brand new service in the shop, and I'm expecting it to double our profits."

"That's good."

"Don't you want to know what it is?"

It would have been difficult for me to have cared any less. "Of course, I do."

"Tanning."

"Sunbeds?"

"No, they're so last year. We've had a spray tan booth installed."

"Aren't they very expensive?"

"Brand new, yes, but we picked this one up from a salon that had gone bust. It was an absolute steal." She looked me up and down. "You always look a little pasty, Jill. You'd look much better with a bit of a tan."

"I don't think so. It's not really my thing."

"Here." She fished something out of her pocket. "This voucher entitles you to fifty percent off on your first visit."

"Thanks, but I really don't—"

"Got to run. My next client is due at any minute. Later, Jill."

***

When I got back from Coffee Games, Kathy and Lizzie were waiting for me in the outer office.

"Have you been skiving off again?" Kathy grinned.

"Chance would be a fine thing. I've been out on business, and Madeline's mother waylaid me on the way back. Apparently, she's had a spray tan booth installed in that nail bar of hers."

"I wouldn't mind getting a spray tan. I'm beginning to look like a ghost." Kathy put her hand over her mouth. "Whoops, I didn't mean to say that word."

"You don't look like any of the ghosts I've seen, Mummy," Lizzie said.

"I thought we'd agreed you weren't going to talk about those?"

"Sorry, but they've all moved out now, anyway. All except for Caroline."

That was my cue to change the subject. "Are you serious about wanting to get a tan? If you are, Deli gave me a fifty percent off voucher. You can have it."

"Are you sure you don't want it?"

"I'm positive."

"Go on, then. There's no point in letting it go to waste. I might go over there later today, after I've taken Lizzie home."

"Look what Mrs V gave me, Auntie Jill." Lizzie held up a bright yellow scarf.

"It's lovely. Anyway, what brings you and Mummy here today?"

"Lizzie has something she wants to ask you," Kathy said. "Don't you, Lizzie?"

"Mummy says because Daddy is fishing with Mikey on Sunday, and Uncle Jack is working away, it would be nice if the three of us could have a girls' day out. Please say yes, Auntie Jill."

"Shopping?" The thought of going shopping with Kathy horrified me.

"No." Kathy shook her head. "Lizzie and I thought the three of us could go to a park, and maybe even take a picnic."

"Will you come, Auntie Jill?" Lizzie took hold of my hand.

"Why not? I don't have anything else planned."

"Yay!" Lizzie bounced up and down with excitement.

Shopping with Kathy would have been a definite no-no, but a relaxing day in the park, with a picnic, sounded like just the ticket to help me unwind after a stressful week.

Just then, a man came into the outer office.

"I'm here about the blinds, love." He was wearing a blue uniform with the company name: None So, on his breast pocket.

"We'll get out of your hair, Jill." Kathy took Lizzie's hand. "We'll pick you up on Saturday morning."

"Okay, see you then." I turned to the man. "Come through to my office, would you?"

"These look like they've seen better days." He cast a professional eye over the old blinds. "How long have they been stuck like that?"

"Not long. A few weeks."

Behind me, on the sofa, Winky laughed. "And the rest."

"Shut it, you!"

"What did you say?" The man glared at me.

"Nothing, I was sneezing. Achoo. It's my hay fever."

"Oh? Right. Anyway, these windows are a standard size, so I can fit the new blinds right now if you like. Two-hundred and ten pounds for the lot. That includes fitting."

"Err—" I glanced at Winky who gave me the paws-up. "That's fine. Please go ahead."

"What colour did you want?"

"Grey if you have them."

"We have every colour under the sun."

"Great. Grey it is, then. Do you need me to be here because I was thinking of calling it a day? My PA will be in the outer office."

"No, that's fine. I'll crack on with them."

On my way out, I brought Mrs V up to speed. "I'm going home now, Mrs V. Are you okay to stay until the man has finished fitting the blinds?"

"Yes, Armi isn't picking me up until just after five. Will the man need paying?"

"No, Winky is—err—I mean, I'll sort that out tomorrow."

Chapter 10

The next morning, over breakfast, I told Jack about Deli's new business venture.

"You should have given me the voucher for the spray tan," he said.

"You're joking."

"Of course I'm joking. Where are you going for the picnic on Sunday?"

"To a park, I think. I'm not sure which one, though. Kathy said she'd come and pick me up."

"It's alright for some. I'm going to be stuck in an office all day."

"It's your own fault. You will insist on leaving me every weekend."

"It isn't through choice, believe me. I'm sick of training courses. It's not like I ever learn anything useful."

As Jack and I were on our way out of the door, my phone rang.

"I'd better take this."

"Okay, see you tonight." He gave me a quick kiss and then headed to his car.

"Jill? It's Charlie Cross."

"Morning, Charlie."

"I hope you don't mind my sticking my oar in, but I've tracked down the lady who used to clean for Myrtle. I thought you might want to talk to her."

"I do, yeah. Do you have her number? I'll call her to see if I can set up a time to go and see her."

"Actually, I've already done that."

"Oh? Okay."

"Her name is Freda Bowling, and she said she'd be happy for you to go over and see her this afternoon at three o'clock if that works for you."

"Yes, that should be okay."

Charlie gave me her details and I promised to keep him posted.

***

"What time did the blinds man get done yesterday, Mrs V?"

"He'd finished by a quarter to five. I must say, I'm rather surprised by the colour you chose."

"What's wrong with grey?"

"Are they supposed to be grey?"

I hurried through to my office, but then stopped dead in my tracks.

"They look good, don't they?" Winky was sitting on my desk, admiring the new blinds.

"They're purple! I told you specifically that I didn't want purple."

"They're not purple. They're grey like you asked for. This particular shade is called Grey au Violet."

"Don't give me any of that rubbish. They're clearly purple."

Just then, my phone rang. It was Desdemona Nightowl, headmistress of CASS; she sounded panic-stricken.

"Ms Nightowl? What's wrong?"

"The most terrible thing has happened. We're marooned. No one can get in or out."

"I'm sorry, but I have no idea what you're talking about."

"That's my fault. I'm so upset by the whole thing I can't think straight. Give me a moment while I take a deep breath."

"Sure."

The line was silent for several minutes, and I was beginning to think we'd been disconnected, but then she said, "Sorry about that, Jill. Have you come across royal dragons before?"

"I don't think so."

"They're only found in and around the White Mountains, which are equidistant between Candlefield and CASS. They're enormous creatures, but usually completely docile. During my tenure, we've had no trouble from them whatsoever, but for some reason, one of them has started to attack the airship."

"I understood from Reggie that the airship flew too high for the dragons to attack it, and that it was fitted with defences that would ward them off."

"That's true, but the royal dragon can fly higher than any other dragon, and it seems to be impervious to the usual defensive measures. As I said before, this has never been a problem in the past because royal dragons were never considered to be a threat."

"Any idea why it should suddenly have become aggressive?"

"None at all, but at the moment, it's impossible to travel either to or from CASS. So far, none of the parents are aware of this issue, but it's half-term in a couple of weeks. If the children are unable to return home then, I won't be able to keep it under wraps."

"What about your supplies?"

"Fortunately, we're well stocked with all the essentials,

so that won't be a problem for a while."

"What exactly do you want me to do, Headmistress?"

"In all honesty, Jill, I'm not sure what you can do, but I didn't know who else to contact."

"I suppose I should start by seeing the problem for myself."

"Do you mean you want to travel on the airship?"

"I don't see any other way. Would the pilot be willing to take me up?"

"If I know Bertie Brownlow, I'm sure he will. Let me give him a call now, and I'll get straight back to you."

"Okay."

Was I completely insane? I'd volunteered to go up in the airship, knowing full well that it was likely to be attacked by a giant dragon.

I couldn't do anything about the blinds now because my head was still spinning from the phone call, so I went through to the outer office.

"Are you alright, Jill?" You look a little dazed.

"Sorry? Err—yes, I'm fine."

My phone rang again.

"Jill, it's Desdemona. I've spoken to Bertie, and he's willing to take you up."

"When?"

"He lives only five minutes from the airship hangar, so he can be there whenever you're ready."

"Okay, but I'll need to make a stop-off in Candlefield first. It shouldn't take long. Will you tell him I'll meet him outside the hangar one hour from now."

"Will do, and Jill—"

"Yes?"

"Good luck."

"Are you sure you're okay, Jill?" Mrs V said. "You look very pale."

"I—err—I think I'll step outside for a breath of fresh air. I won't be long."

When would I ever learn? Of all the things I'd volunteered for, taking a trip in an airship to see an angry dragon had to be by far the most stupid. But, I was committed now, so I had to at least make sure I was forearmed. I wanted to find out as much as I could about the royal dragon, and I knew exactly where to find the information I needed.

"Jill?" Deloris Shuttlebug answered her door, wearing an apron and rubber gloves. "What a lovely surprise. You must forgive the way I look. I was in the middle of my weekly clean."

"I'm sorry to trouble you Deloris, but I wondered if you had your husband's manuscript here, or is it with the publisher?"

"They took a copy. I still have the original upstairs."

"Do you think I could take a look at it, please. It'll only take me a few minutes."

"Of course, come in. Would you like a drink?"

"No, thanks. I can't stay long—there's somewhere I have to be."

Cuthbert Shuttlebug had devoted a whole section of his book to dragons. The illustration of the destroyer dragon was uncannily accurate and sent a shiver down my spine. The royal dragon was a much more handsome creature, and well-deserving of its name. Although as large as the destroyer, it was, according to Cuthbert, a much more placid animal. Reclusive, it avoided contact with other creatures, and rarely if ever used one of its main weapons: the ability to breathe fire. Gulp. I had hoped this particular dragon wouldn't be of the fire-breathing variety.

I put the manuscript back on the shelf, and hurried back downstairs.

"Thanks, Deloris."

"Did you get everything you needed?"

"Yes, thanks. That was very helpful."

From there, I magicked myself over to the hangar where a man, dressed in a grey uniform and matching grey cap, was waiting outside the building. He didn't look even a tiny bit nervous.

"Mr Brownlow?"

"Call me BeeBee, everyone does. You must be the great Jill Gooder. I've heard a lot about you."

"It's actually Jill Maxwell now. I got married recently."

"Drat." He grinned. "And there was me hoping for a date later."

BeeBee looked at least seventy, and was probably several centuries older, but the twinkle in his eye suggested he'd once been quite the ladies' man.

"I have to say, BeeBee, you don't seem at all nervous."

"Why would I be? I've piloted this old girl a thousand times."

"I was thinking more about the dragon."

"It'll take more than a dragon to kill off old BeeBee."

"Have you actually seen it?"

"I have. I was taking some supplies over to CASS when the brute attacked. There was no getting past it, so I was forced to turn around and head back here."

"Couldn't you take a different route around the dragon?"

"It's not that easy. The wind currents between here and CASS can be lethal. The route we take is the only safe one. What's your plan today, Jill?"

"I wish I had one. As I told the headmistress, I thought I should start by seeing first-hand what was happening."

"In that case, why don't I up-anchor and get us underway?"

The pilot's cabin was located below the main passenger deck, so once we were airborne, the only way I could communicate with BeeBee was through the intercom.

"How much longer, BeeBee?" I asked when we'd been airborne for about fifteen minutes.

"The last time we tried to make the journey, the beast appeared as we were crossing the White Mountains. We're about five minutes away from there now."

"Okay. Let's both keep our eyes peeled."

"Don't worry. If it decides to check us out, you'll know about it. It's enormous."

"Over there, to the right, those are the White Mountains," BeeBee called out. "If it's going to—" He didn't get to finish the sentence because the dragon suddenly appeared, and it was headed straight for us. "Hold tight, Jill!"

I didn't need telling twice. I grabbed the handrail and held on for dear life.

The dragon was even bigger than I'd imagined, and it was on a collision course with us.

"Brace yourself, Jill! It's going to hit us!"

BeeBee had no sooner got the words out than a powerful impact knocked the airship to one side.

"We have to go back, Jill."

"Okay." I wasn't about to argue.

While BeeBee turned the airship around, I never once took my eyes off the dragon. If it decided to attack again, and caught us full-on this time, it would be curtains. Fortunately, it seemed content to watch from a distance, as we headed back to Candlefield.

"That was a bit hairy," BeeBee said, once we were back on solid ground.

"Is that what happened the last time?"

"More or less."

"That only felt like a warning shot to me. If it had wanted to, it could easily have taken us down. A head-on impact would have wiped us out, but it seemed to deliberately give us only a glancing blow."

"I think we were just lucky, Jill."

"I don't think so. The royal dragon can breathe fire. If it had wanted to take us out, why didn't it burn us to a crisp? And why did it only attack the once? As soon as it saw that we'd turned around, it backed off."

"You could be right, but one thing's for sure. While that monster is around, there'll be no airships going between here and CASS. What's your plan now?"

"I don't have one yet, but I think I should go and update the headmistress."

"How are you going to do that without the—Oh, wait, I remember now. You can magic yourself there, can't you?

Well, good luck. I hope you manage to sort that dragon out, otherwise I'm going to be out of a job."

"I'll do my best. Thanks for everything, BeeBee."

***

After magicking myself to CASS, I updated the headmistress on my aborted airship journey.

"I really don't think it was trying to destroy us, headmistress. If it had wanted to, it could have crushed the airship and made charcoal out of us."

"You may be right, but that doesn't alter the fact that we're effectively marooned here."

"I want to go to the White Mountains to get a closer look at the dragon."

"That would be suicide."

"Not necessarily. I've battled and defeated dragons before, using my magic."

"I know you're powerful, Jill, but the royal dragon is not just any old dragon."

"Do you have any other suggestions?"

"No, but I simply can't ask you to risk your life like this."

"You didn't ask; I volunteered."

"If you insist on going, you can't go alone. Have you heard of the protectors?"

"Some of the pupils mentioned them the other day. Aren't they the wizards who accompany the kids when they go on field trips?"

"That's right. There are three of them here at the moment. They're marooned like the rest of us. Goodness knows how much their bill will be when they're eventually able to get back to Candlefield. If we're paying them anyway, they might as well earn their keep by accompanying you."

"Do you think they'll agree to do that?"

"I don't know. It's over and above their contract, but I can ask them."

"Okay, but the sooner we get this show on the road, the better."

Chapter 11

"I'm Hardy, head of this group of reprobates." The man-mountain gestured to the two men standing behind him.

The protectors had apparently needed no persuading to accompany me on the trip to the White Mountains.

"I've never killed a royal dragon before," Hardy said. "Should be a fun trip."

"I'm not sure about that, but I'm pleased to have you on board. One thing, though, I don't want to kill the dragon unless we have no other choice."

"You're the boss. Your call."

"Okay. Let's do this."

Before we set off, the headmistress provided me with a change of clothing. The safari suit was unflattering, but I was soon thankful for it, as we fought our way through the incredibly thick undergrowth.

"How long will it take us, Hardy?"

"I reckon it's a couple of hours' walk from here." He checked his compass. "More if the undergrowth is as bad as this all the way."

"Have you been to the White Mountains before?"

"Never, and I don't know anyone who has. The furthest we normally go is the Valley of Shadows when we're accompanying the kids on their field trips. That only takes around thirty minutes."

Fighting my way through the undergrowth was bad enough, but it was the heat that sapped almost every ounce of my energy.

"How much further?" I asked for the umpteenth time, like a kid on their way to the seaside.

"We're almost there." He pointed. "Do you see those peaks? Those are the White Mountains. Another ten minutes, and we should be at their base."

It was actually closer to twenty minutes later when we emerged from the forest. It was great to finally be free of all the annoying insects, which had been buzzing around my face for the last couple of hours.

"The dragon's nest is likely to be high in the mountains," Hardy said. "Hopefully, we can surprise it while it's asleep. It doesn't look a particularly difficult climb."

Not difficult for him and his men, maybe, but there was no way I'd be able to get up there in my current state of exhaustion.

"Help!" The voice came from somewhere above us. "We're trapped!"

Although I could hear them, I couldn't see anyone.

"Where are you?" Hardy shouted. "Show yourself."

"Up here!"

"Look! Over there!" I pointed to a makeshift white flag, which was being waved by a small elf-like figure who was kneeling on a ledge.

"Can't you get down?" I shouted.

"We daren't. Every time we try to make a move, the dragon attacks us."

"When did you last see it?"

"Earlier today."

"It seems to be all clear now. Why not try —"

First, I saw the shadow, and then I heard the sound of the creature's giant wings.

Hardy and his men rushed for cover in the small cave at the base of the mountain. I started to follow, but quickly realised I'd never make it, so I did a U-turn and headed back for the cover of the forest. Once there, I looked up at the ledge, but there was no sign of the elf-like figure. Hopefully, he'd taken shelter somewhere.

Meanwhile, the dragon had landed in the clearing, close to the cave where Hardy and his men were sheltering. If it breathed fire into the cave, the three of them would be toast. I had to distract the creature somehow.

"Hey, you!" I stepped out from the cover of the forest. "Over here!"

The dragon turned its head towards me, and I was expecting the worst, but then it spoke in a gentle voice, "What kind of creature are you?"

"I'm a witch."

"How come I can understand what you're saying?"

"I don't know. I can speak to some animals, but I had no idea I'd be able to talk to you until just now."

It began to walk slowly towards me, and there was something about its demeanour and tone of voice that told me I wasn't in danger, so instead of turning tail and running, I stood my ground.

"I'm a conquestor dragon."

"Oh? I thought you were a royal dragon?"

"No, I'm definitely a conquestor. My name is Sybil."

"I'm Jill. Nice to meet you, Sybil."

"Likewise. Why have you come here?"

"I came to find you."

"Me? Why?"

"It's a little awkward. I wanted to find out why you've been attacking the airship."

"What's an airship?"

"It's—err—it's like a giant bird, I suppose. It flies across these mountains."

"Do you mean the flying creature which makes the strange noise?"

"Yeah, that's it."

"I had to keep it away from Cora."

"Who's Cora?"

"My baby. She's in the nest. Would you like to see her?"

"Where exactly is your nest?"

"Up there, near the top. Hop on my back and I'll take you up there."

"I—err—I'm really not sure about this."

"Come on. You'll be perfectly safe."

"Okay." I scrambled up her tail, and then sat astride her back.

"Are you ready, Jill?"

"As ready as I'll ever be." I held on for dear life as she began to flap her huge wings. Moments later, we were soaring through the air.

"Cora, this is Jill." Sybil had put me down next to a giant nest, which contained the cutest little dragon you ever did see.

"Kip, kip," Cora said.

"That's all she can say." The proud mother looked on.

"She's gorgeous."

"She is, isn't she? But then, I'm biased."

"Did you attack the airship, err—flying creature because you thought it might harm your baby?"

"Yes. Cora is my first, so I can't take any chances. I didn't really attack it, though; I just chased it away. Like I did with those funny little creatures on the ledge below."

"Funny little—? Oh, you mean the elves."

"I thought they might come after Cora."

"I don't blame you for being protective towards your baby, but the flying creature isn't actually a creature at all."

"It looks like one to me."

"I can see how it would, but it's actually a—err—it's difficult to explain. We use it to travel around in. It won't do any harm to you or your baby."

"Are you sure?"

"You brought me up here to see Cora, so I'm guessing you trust me."

"Yes, you seem nice."

"Thanks. Could I ask a favour of you?"

"Sure."

"Would you allow the airship to fly over these mountains? I give you my word that no harm will come to you or Cora."

"Okay, but what about those funny little creatures on the ledge? What did you call them?"

"Elves. At least I think that's what they are. If you take me to the ledge where they're hiding, I'll make sure they leave here without causing you any problems. Is that a deal?"

"It's a deal."

"Great."

"Get back on board, and I'll take you down there now."

I did as she said, and as we flew away, I waved goodbye to Cora.

"Kip, kip."

***

Sybil dropped me off close to the ledge where I'd seen the elf.

"Thanks, Sybil."

"My pleasure. Are you sure you don't want me to stick around to take you all the way down?"

"No, it's okay. I should be able to get down from here."

I waited until she'd flown away, and then went in search of the elf. It was only when I began to inch my way along the ledge that I spotted the entrance to a tiny cave. It was much too small for me to get in, but I knelt down and looked inside. Huddled there were four tiny elves who all looked terrified.

"Hi, in there. It's safe now. You can come out."

"Are you sure?" The one with the makeshift flag took a few steps forward. "What about the dragon?"

"She's gone, and she's promised not to hurt you as long as you leave this side of the mountain."

"What do you mean, she *promised*? How can a dragon make you a promise?"

"It's a long story; too long to go into now. You're just going to have to trust me."

"I'm not sure about this."

"It's up to you, obviously, but the alternative is to stay in that cave for the rest of your lives, which probably won't be very long without food or water."

He turned to the others, and they exchanged a few words.

"Okay. We're coming out."

They all looked terrified, and kept checking the sky, in case the dragon returned.

"How did you get here from Candlefield?"

"We don't come from Candlefield. We live on the other side of the mountains in a small village called Evkon."

"I didn't think anyone lived out here."

"We're the only ones as far as I know. Our ancestors moved to the White Mountains to find work, and they decided to stay."

"What kind of work?"

"We're miners."

"What is it that you mine?"

"Blue star crystals. Every few years, some of us make the expedition to Candlefield to sell them for cash, or to exchange them for the goods we need. Otherwise, we pretty much live off the land."

"Where are the mines located?"

"On the other side of this mountain range. We only came over here to see what the prospects were like for possible future development. That's when the dragon attacked us. We were taken totally by surprise because we've lived close to these dragons for ages, and we've never had any problems before."

"There's a reason for that. This one has a young baby, and she thought you meant her harm."

"We would never hurt anyone."

"I believe you, but you'll have to stay clear of this side of the mountain, at least until the baby dragon has grown up."

"Don't worry. We won't be back here in a hurry. You'd better come with us—getting down this slope can be very dangerous."

"I'll be fine. You go ahead. I'm going to rest up a while before I attempt it."

"Are you sure?"

"I'm positive. I'll be okay."

"I don't even know your name."

"It's Jill. Jill Maxwell."

"I'm Cyrus. If there's ever anything we can do to help you, you know where we are."

"Thanks."

I waited until the elves were out of sight, and then magicked myself to ground level.

What? You didn't actually think I was going to climb down, did you?

I landed just outside the cave where Hardy and his men had taken refuge.

"Hardy! Are you in there? It's safe to come out now."

Moments later, the three of them appeared from the shadows.

"Where's the dragon?" Hardy said.

"It's okay. Sybil won't do us any harm."

"*Sybil?*"

"That's her name; she was only trying to chase us off to protect her baby."

"How can you know that?"

I told him about my visit to the dragon's nest, and her promise not to attack the airship again.

"I'm not sure you actually needed our protection, Jill. It seems to me you are quite capable of looking after yourself."

"I still appreciate you accompanying me here. I'm not sure I would have found it without you."

"Are you ready for the long trek home?"

"Actually, I'm going to make my own way back. I know

a shortcut."

"There is no shortcut. None that I know of, anyway."

"That's where you're wrong. I'll see you guys back there."

Now that I had my bearings, there was no sense in putting myself through the ordeal of the forest again, so instead, I simply magicked myself back to CASS.

"Jill? Thank goodness you're okay." The headmistress ushered me into her office. "You look exhausted."

"I'm fine. Just about."

"Where are the others?"

"They're okay too, but they're taking the long road home."

"What happened out there?"

"I have good news: The dragon won't attack the airship again."

"Did you kill it?"

"No, that wasn't necessary. She's actually very friendly. Her name is Sybil."

"You *spoke* to a royal dragon? I didn't think that was possible."

"Yes, and the first thing I discovered was that they're actually conquestor dragons. At least, that's what they call themselves, and I guess they should know. The only reason she attacked the airship was to protect her baby. Now that I've explained she has nothing to fear from it, she's promised to leave it alone."

"Do you think we can trust her?"

"I'm absolutely sure of it."

"That's excellent news. Once again, we are in your debt, Jill."

"No problem. It was my pleasure, but I'd better get back now."

***

"Do you feel better for that walk in the fresh air, Jill?" Mrs V looked up and did a double take. "What on earth are you wearing, and what is that awful smell?"

Oh bum! I'd forgotten to get changed, so I was still wearing the safari suit.

"This? I saw it in a charity shop and couldn't resist it."

"You'd think they would have washed it before they put it out for sale."

"Yes, well, I'd better crack on. Lots to do." I hurried through to my office.

"What on earth have you come as?" Winky laughed.

"It's a safari suit."

He put a paw over his nose. "You smell like a sweaty old sock."

He was right—I did. I should have showered and changed before leaving CASS.

"So, Smelly?" He edged as far away from me as he could get. "About these blinds?"

"What about them?"

"Are you going to insist I get them changed?"

"What? No, they'll do."

"Just like that? After all the fuss you made before?"

"After what I've just been through, I've realised that blinds aren't all that important in the scheme of things."

"*All you've been through?* Do me a favour. You've literally only been gone for five minutes."

"I've explained before that time stands still in this world

while I'm in the sup world. Since I last saw you, I've taken a ride on an airship that was attacked by a dragon. I walked miles through a jungle in search of that dragon, and then I flew on its back to its nest where I met its baby. Then I rescued some elf miners who were trapped on the mountainside. Not bad for a morning's work, even if I do say so myself."

"That's all very commendable, I'm sure, but it doesn't alter the fact that you're stinking the place out. Don't they have showers in this other world of yours?"

Chapter 12

There was no way I could sit in the office all afternoon, dressed in a safari suit, and smelling like a sweaty old sock. As Winky had so delicately put it. I couldn't drive home like this because the car would have needed fumigating afterwards.

"Winky."

"Yes, Smelly?"

"I'm going to use magic to go home, get showered and change."

"Thank goodness for that. That smell is making me quite nauseous."

"I shouldn't be very long."

"What if the old bag lady comes looking for you?"

"You'll have to cover for me."

"And how am I supposed to do that?"

"You're a smart cat; you'll figure it out."

Once home, I put the safari suit and my underwear straight into a large black plastic bag that I found on the kitchen worktop. After dropping it outside the door, I hurried upstairs for a much-needed shower.

Boy, that felt good. It was great to have finally got rid of the smell of the forest. I was sitting on the bed, wrapped in a towel, drying my hair when there was a loud knock at the door. It was most likely someone selling something, so I ignored it. They knocked again, even louder this time. And then again. Whoever was at the door wasn't going away, so I quickly threw on some clothes and went downstairs.

"What do you call this?" A red-faced woman held up

the black plastic bag.

"Sorry?"

"I'm sick and tired of you people, thinking that you can use us to get rid of your dirty washing." She pinched her nose. "It smells like something crawled in here and died."

"Sorry? Do I know you? Why are you holding my rubbish?"

"There!" She exploded. "You've admitted it. You were trying to foist your smelly rubbish on us."

"I have no idea what you're talking about. I've just this minute dropped that bag outside. I was going to put it in the dustbin later."

"Then why did you use *our* bag?" She spun the bag around, and for the first time, I noticed the white lettering printed on the bottom. It read: Washbridge Clothes Aid – a registered charity.

"Sorry, I didn't realise it was your bag. I thought it was just a regular waste bag."

"Really? Do you know how much it costs us to have these bags printed? And how much it costs to distribute them door-to-door, and then to collect the clothes that have been donated? A small fortune, that's how much."

"Look, this really is just a big misunderstanding. Maybe, I—err—perhaps, I could give you a small donation?"

"How small?"

"Wait there while I go and get my purse." This was all Jack's fault. How was I supposed to know the bag he'd left lying around in the kitchen was a charity collection bag? "I only have two twenty-pound notes and loose change."

"That will do."

I started to count out the coins. "Fifty-pence, seventy-pence—"

"I meant the notes."

"But that's all the cash I have on me."

"Do you know how much money I stand to lose today? I can't continue on my collection while I smell like this. I'll have to go home to shower and change." She hesitated. "Unless, of course—" She glanced over my shoulder.

"Do you mean you want to take a shower here?"

"Would you mind? It is your fault I'm in this predicament."

"I suppose not."

"Great." She snatched the two banknotes from my hand, and then stepped into the house. "We're about the same size. Maybe you have some clothes I could change into?"

By the time she'd showered, and changed into my favourite summer dress, it felt like the two of us were old friends.

"I'm sorry again for the mix-up, Maggie," I said, as I showed her out.

"That's okay, but I still can't imagine what possessed you to buy that safari suit."

"It's a long story."

"You have my card, so don't forget what I said. We're always on the lookout for people to help with these collections. Give me a call if you have any spare time."

"I will. Bye, then."

***

"You took your sweet time," Winky said when I landed back in the office. "I was beginning to think you'd been overcome by the fumes and died."

"I had a charity-bag mix-up situation."

"A what?"

"It doesn't matter. Mrs V didn't come looking for me, did she?"

"She did as it happens, but don't worry, I covered for you, just like you asked me to."

"Right? And how did you manage—no, never mind. It's better I don't know."

I'd just finished rearranging my paperclip drawer when Mrs V popped her head around the door. "Is it safe to come in now?"

"Of course. Why wouldn't it be?"

"Has that cat finished with the funny turn?"

"Err, yeah, he's fine. It's perfectly safe to come in."

Without once taking her gaze off Winky, she took a few tentative steps into the office. "This is getting beyond a joke, Jill. It's coming to something when I daren't come into your office for fear of being attacked."

"*Attacked?*" I glared at Winky.

"You must have seen what he did when I tried to come in a few minutes ago?"

"Err, yeah, but I wouldn't call that an attack."

"What would you call it, then?"

"He was only being playful."

"*Playful?* If I hadn't got out of here when I did, he would have ripped me to shreds."

"Honestly, Mrs V, you really don't have to be scared of Winky. He wouldn't hurt a fly, would you, boy?"

Right on cue, he began to purr.

"I still say there's something seriously wrong with that cat." Mrs V allowed herself to look away from him for the first time. "What happened to your safari suit?"

Oh bum!

"I — err — nipped home a while back and got changed."

"I didn't see you leave or come back."

"You had your head on the desk, napping, so I didn't like to disturb you."

"I did? Oh deary me. But then, I haven't been sleeping very well recently. It must be the stress of the driving lessons."

"Don't worry about it, Mrs V. It's all good."

"Okay, dear, but I still think you should get rid of that cat."

I waited until she'd closed the door, and then let Winky have both barrels. "What were you thinking? Why did you attack her?"

"You told me to cover for you!"

"I didn't say you should attack her."

"She's being a drama queen as per usual. It's like you said, I was only being playful. And anyway, how else was I supposed to cover for you? I'm a cat, remember?"

He had a point.

***

Later that afternoon, I had an unexpected visit from my mother, which sent Winky scurrying for cover under the sofa.

"I don't think your cat likes me," she observed.

"I wouldn't take it personally. He's not a big fan of ghosts."

"I wish you wouldn't call me that."

"Ghost?"

"Yes, I much prefer spirit."

"But you live in *Ghost* Town."

"You do realise that isn't its real name, don't you? It's actually called Grande Tramagne, but some idiot shortened that to GT, and then some other idiots decided it would be funny to say that GT stood for Ghost Town. And from that point on, the original name fell into disuse."

"Now you mention it, I do seem to remember someone told me the real name."

"That someone would be me."

"I suppose it must have been."

"I intend to campaign for the old name to be brought back."

"Good luck with that."

"I thought I'd pop over because I have a couple of things to tell you."

"Okay?"

"First, I wanted to update you on the Ghost Horizons situation. I had a word with Constance Bowler, and she set up a sting, like you suggested. I'm pleased to report that the charlatans who ran that business are now behind bars."

"That's great news."

"Yes, but it means that we're still looking for somewhere we can holiday in the human world. You will keep a lookout for anywhere that might be suitable, won't you?"

"Absolutely. What was the other thing you wanted to tell me?"

"I wanted to invite you to a party to celebrate our wedding anniversary."

"I didn't think it was yours and Alberto's anniversary for ages yet?"

"It isn't. I'm talking about mine and your father's wedding anniversary."

"Hold on. You and my father are no longer married – at least, not to one another."

"That doesn't alter the fact that it's the anniversary of the day on which we got married."

"I'm sorry, Mum, but that is possibly the most ridiculous thing I've ever heard. What do Alberto and Blodwyn think about it?"

"They enjoy a good party as much as anyone."

"They may do, but I can't help but feel they might be a little peeved at the idea of their partners celebrating the anniversary of their previous marriage. Have you actually asked them how they feel?"

"Yes, err – well, not in so many words, but Alberto would say if he wasn't happy. And Blodwyn isn't one to keep quiet if she has something to say. Anyway, it's all organised now. You will come, won't you?"

"When is it?"

"In a couple of weeks at the Grand Tramagne Social Club."

"I thought you'd just have a small get-together at your place."

"It wouldn't be big enough. Not for the number of people we've invited. It's a pity you can't bring Jack with you."

"Yeah, well that's never going to happen, is it?"

"But you'll be there?"

"I guess so."

"Great. It starts at eight." She gave me a ghostly peck on the cheek. "I'd better get back because I've left Alberto peeling the onions."

"Bye, Mum."

***

Freda Bowling lived in Little Bigging, a village located some ten miles from Middle Tweaking. She answered the door with curlers in her hair. Two curlers, to be precise. I suspected that she'd somehow managed to miss those two when removing the rest, and I wondered if I should say something. In the end, I decided against it, but Freda must have seen me staring at them because she said, "You're probably wondering about the curlers?"

"Err, no, I hadn't even noticed them."

"They won't all fit on my head at the same time— my head's too small, so I have to do it in two parts. I put the majority of them in, and then when they're done, I put in the two which I didn't have enough room for the first time around."

"I see." Oh boy! "Charlie Cross said you wanted to talk to me about Myrtle."

"That's right."

"I was sorry to hear what had happened to her. Why don't you come through to the lounge while I make us both a cup of tea?"

Once we had our drinks, I tried to focus on the interview, but it wasn't easy because my gaze kept being drawn to those two curlers.

"Charlie told me that you cleaned for Myrtle for a while."

"That's right. Just while she was laid up with a bad ankle."

"How did you feel when Myrtle let you go?"

"It wasn't a problem. I always knew it was a temporary arrangement, and besides, Middle Tweaking is too far away for me to take on work there on a permanent basis. Most of my regulars live in and around this village."

"Do you have a car?"

"No, I can't drive. I take the bus everywhere."

"How did Myrtle come to contact you in the first place?"

"A friend of a friend. Gina Bailey, who lives here in Little Bigging, recommended me to a friend of Myrtle's. If it had been a permanent position, I'd have turned it down, but I knew I'd be able to cope for a few weeks, and the extra cash came in handy."

"Did you have a key?"

"Yes, in fact I still have it. I tried to give it back to Myrtle, but she said I should hang onto it in case she needed me again at some future date."

"Did you ever see any strangers hanging around the house while you were working there?"

"No, but then I had my head down, working, most of the time."

"Did you know Rob Evans?"

"I don't think so, but then I don't know many of them by name."

The two curlers were still in place when I took my leave.

Chapter 13

Jack and I had a lovely day together on Saturday. We did a little shopping in the morning, grabbed lunch, and then, as it had started to rain, we went to the movies. It was ages since I'd been to the cinema, and I thoroughly enjoyed it, even if the popcorn and drink did cost more than the cinema tickets. The only thing that spoiled an otherwise perfect day was that Jack had to leave straight after dinner because he was staying overnight at the hotel, ahead of his course on Sunday.

The next morning, I woke up at the crack of dawn, and was about to roll over and go back to sleep when I remembered that I'd promised to go on a picnic with Kathy and Lizzie.

I know what you're thinking: Jill's going to moan again. Well, you're wrong. The sun was already shining through the bedroom window, so a picnic in the park sounded like the ideal way to spend my Sunday. I had a spring in my step, as I jumped out of bed, showered and got dressed.

What? Okay, I lied about the *spring in my step* part.

Kathy had said we'd take her car, but rather than have her come out to Smallwash and then drive back into town, I'd said I'd take my car to her house, and leave it there. As I set off, there wasn't a cloud in the sky, the birds were singing, and there was no sign of Mr Ivers. The perfect start to what promised to be a fantastic day.

What the —?

I couldn't believe my eyes. Daubed on the bridge were the words: JILL IS A WITCH. They'd been painted on the opposite side from the previous occasion.

"When did this happen?" I said to the young man in the toll booth who, judging by the hair-free skin below his nose, had given up on the moustache.

"When did *what* happen?"

"The graffiti!"

"Oh yeah. It was like that when I got here this morning."

"What about the guy who worked the nightshift?"

"Gordy? He said he didn't see who did it. He was probably — err."

"Asleep? Again? It's just not good enough. If he's being paid to work the nightshift, he should be awake."

The young guy shrugged. "I can give you a form to complete if you want to make an official complaint."

"Would it do any good?"

"It doesn't usually."

"What's your name?"

"Me? I'm Chris, but everyone calls me Cheesy, on account of my surname."

"Don't tell me; let me guess. Is it Wensleydale?"

"No."

"Leicester, then?"

"No."

"Camembert?"

"You'll never get it. It's actually Board. Chris Board."

"I don't get it — oh, hang on. Cheeseboard?"

"Yeah."

Wow! Just wow!

"O — kay, anyway, we have to put a stop to this graffiti."

"I was going to call head office to get it removed."

"Don't bother. That'll take forever. I'll see to it, but I do need you to do something for me." I took out a pen, grabbed a scrap of paper from the glove compartment, and wrote down my phone number. "Call me on this number if you see anyone putting up more graffiti."

"Okay, but like I said, it usually happens at night when Gordy's working."

"Will you see Gordy tonight?"

"Yeah. I have to hand over to him."

"In that case, tell him that I work for the council, and I'm going to be making spot checks. If I catch him asleep, I'll make sure he's fired. And give him my number. Okay?"

"Yeah, I'll tell him."

***

On the drive over to Kathy's, I pulled into a lay-by and phoned Tatts. I didn't hold out much hope of being able to contact him on a Sunday morning, but he answered first time. He proudly informed me that his business operated twenty-four seven, three hundred and sixty-five days a year, and that he would be happy to remove the fresh graffiti for the same price as last time. I agreed, and he promised that it would be gone before I came home that afternoon. This whole graffiti thing was costing me an arm and a leg. The sooner I found out who was behind it, and put a stop to it, the better.

I'd just parked my car outside Kathy's house when Lizzie came running down the drive to greet me.

"Auntie Jill, Auntie Jill, Mummy is orange."

"*Orange?*"

"You mustn't say anything because she'll get angry. Daddy said we should pretend like she isn't."

"Right. I won't say —" Just then, Kathy came out of the house, and I dissolved into laughter.

"Don't you dare laugh!" She wagged her finger at me. "This is all your fault."

"How is it *my* fault? It's not like I *oranged* it." I lost it again.

"Lizzie, go and get in the car. Auntie Jill and I need to have a quick chat." Kathy waited until Lizzie was in the back seat, and then she turned on me again. "Why did you let me go through with it?"

"You said you wanted a tan."

"I know I did, but I didn't want to end up looking like this. There must be something wrong with their equipment."

"Deli did say they'd picked it up cheap, second-hand."

"And you didn't think to mention that?"

"I had no reason to believe it was faulty. And anyway, it doesn't look all that bad." If you're colour blind.

"If I hadn't promised Lizzie that the three of us would go out today, I'd lock myself away until this faded."

"No one will even notice, I promise. And if they do, tell them you did it for a bet."

"You're really pushing your luck now, Jill."

"Sorry. Which park are we going to?"

"Washbridge Park."

"Can I tell her now, Mummy?" Lizzie shouted from the back seat after we'd been driving for a while.

"Not yet. It'll be a nice surprise for Auntie Jill."

"Tell me what?" I was beginning to smell a rat—an

orange one. "What surprise?"

"Please, Mummy, can I tell her?"

"Okay, then. We're almost there anyway."

"It's the Clownathon!" Lizzie blurted out. "In the park today."

My blood ran cold, as I remembered the flyers that I'd seen in and around Washbridge. There were to be events all around the town, but the main focus was in Washbridge Park. That explained why there was so much traffic as we got closer.

"You tricked me, Kathy!"

"How did I trick you? I said we were going for a picnic in the park, and that's what we're doing."

"You never mentioned the Clownathon."

"Didn't I?" She smirked. "I could have sworn I had."

"Mummy says you're scared of clowns, Auntie Jill."

"Your mummy is joking. Of course I'm not scared of them."

"Not much." Kathy said under her breath.

"How could you do this to me?"

"You surely don't expect me to feel bad, do you? Not when you're responsible for me being this ridiculous shade of brown."

"You're not brown; you're orange!"

***

There was so much interest in the Clownathon that we had to leave the car a quarter of a mile from the park. Kathy and I carried the picnic basket between us while Lizzie walked a few paces ahead.

"Whereabouts shall we go?" Lizzie had stopped just

inside the park gates.

"Let's go over there, near those trees." I pointed to the far side of the park.

"You're only suggesting that because there aren't any clowns over there," Kathy said.

"Not at all. I just thought it would be nice to have the shade from those trees. It looks like it will get hot later. Come on, quick, before someone beats us to it." I began to drag Kathy in that direction.

"It's nice here, isn't it?" I sat down on the blanket that Kathy had brought with her.

"Where are the clowns, Mummy?" Lizzie looked all around.

"They're over the other side of the park, Pumpkin."

"Can I go and see them?"

"Of course you can. Maybe Auntie Jill would like to take you?"

"No, it's okay," I said. "You two go and enjoy yourselves. I don't mind staying here to guard the picnic basket."

Kathy shot me a look, but she didn't argue. She took Lizzie's hand and led her towards clown-aggedon.

Despite my initial reservations, the day was turning out to be okay after all. The weather was gorgeous, the spot I'd chosen was quite peaceful, and best of all, there wasn't a clown to be seen.

I really shouldn't have had that second cup of tea before I left the house. Kathy and Lizzie had been gone for almost two hours, and I was now bursting for a pee. I daren't leave the picnic basket unguarded, but I couldn't take it with me. I suppose I could have used magic to hide it, but there were more people around now, and I was afraid someone might see. I was beginning to think I might have to nip into the trees when Kathy and Lizzie came back.

"I thought you two had got lost. I'm bursting for a pee."

"Oh dear. If I'd known—" Kathy grinned. "We'd have stayed away even longer. Right, Lizzie, let's get those sandwiches and cakes out of the basket."

"Don't eat them all while I'm gone," I shouted over my shoulder as I rushed away.

Thankfully, there had only been a short queue for the toilets. And now, I'd better get back before those two had eaten everything.

"Ho, ho, ho!" A tall clown jumped out in front of me.

"Excuse me, please." I tried to sidestep him, but he blocked my way.

"Why, what did you do?" A second, shorter clown appeared behind me. "Ha, ha, ha."

Oh no! I was trapped in a clown sandwich.

"Do you like my flower?" The first clown pointed to a red rose on his lapel.

"Yes, it's very—what the?" I was hit in the face with a jet of water. "That's not funny!"

"Come on, Jill. It really is." The tall clown's voice had changed to one I recognised.

"Daze?"

"Sorry about the water, but we have to stay in character."

"That's okay." I wiped my face. "What are you doing here?"

"We're on the trail of a wicked witch." This time it was the shorter clown's voice I recognised.

"Blaze? How come you two are working together again? Where's Laze?"

"I had to let him go," Daze said. "The guy was two levels beyond useless."

"Are you two back together on a temporary basis, then?"

"No, it's permanent," Daze said.

"Like the good old days, then?"

"Not quite." Blaze was quick to correct me. "It's an equal partnership now, isn't it, Daze?"

"Hmm." She didn't sound very enthusiastic.

"I thought you were trying to track down the source of the contaminated blood?"

"We are, but we're shorthanded again, so we've had to drop that case for today."

"What's the story with the wicked witch?"

"She's actually an old friend of yours, Jill."

"Are you talking about the one who was running the sweet shop in Washbridge?"

"None other. The infamous Edna Eyesore."

"But you arrested her. Why isn't she behind bars?"

"She was, but there was a jailbreak a couple of weeks back. I'm surprised you didn't hear about it."

"I assume she's up to her old tricks?"

"Of course. Tempting kids with treats, and then turning them into treacle tarts."

"I thought it was gingerbread."

"It usually is, but Edna is on a treacle tart kick at the moment."

"Why would she come here today?"

"Why do you think?" Daze gestured to the dozens of little children who were running around. "Easy pickings for someone like Edna."

"Is there anything I can do to help?"

"Keep your eyes peeled, and if you spot her, give us a shout. She'll no doubt be disguised as a clown, so she won't be easy to pick out."

"Will do."

"Nice to see you again, Jill." Blaze offered his hand.

Instinctively, I shook it, but then quickly pulled away after receiving an electric shock.

"Sorry." He chuckled. "But like Daze said, we have to stay in character."

Still laughing, the two of them walked away. And people wondered why I hated clowns.

Much more worrying, though, was the thought of the wicked witch, ready to prey on all of those innocent children. I would have to keep a very close eye on Lizzie, even if that meant I'd have to mix with the clowns.

Chapter 14

As I headed back to Kathy and Lizzie, I realised that there were two figures standing next to them.

Clowns!

I was about to turn tail and go and hide when Lizzie spotted me.

"Auntie Jill! Come and see the clowns!"

Oh bum! There was no way I could make a run for it now without looking like a total wuss.

"Yes, come and say hello to them, Jill." My orange sister was enjoying this way too much.

"Hi," I said while keeping as much distance between me and the freaky clowns as possible.

"We already know your auntie," one of the clowns said to Lizzie.

"Yes, we actually live across the road from her." The other squeezed his red nose, making Lizzie squeal with laughter.

"Jimmy? Kimmy? I didn't realise it was you."

"Sneezy and Breezy, if you don't mind." Breezy corrected me. "We're on duty."

"Sorry."

Sneezy gave a huge sneeze, which blew her hat off, and sent Lizzie into convulsions of laughter.

When Sneezy bent down to collect her hat, Breezy gave her a kick up the backside with his oversize shoes. That sent both Kathy and Lizzie into hysterics.

Not me, though. I looked on incredulously. How did anyone find this stuff amusing? And that's when I remembered that I'd sponsored these two clowns.

"Excuse me, Breezy."

"Yes, Jill?"

"This sponsorship thing. How does it work exactly?"

"You pay us for every laugh that registers on the clownometer."

"Where is the clownometer?"

"Right here." He rolled up his sleeve.

Sneezy did likewise.

They each had a small gadget, which resembled a Fitbit, strapped to their wrist.

"They can't actually register laughs, though, can they?" I said.

"Sure they can. Watch this." Breezy held out his wrist so I could see the small screen.

Sneezy sneezed again (she was apparently a one-trick pony), sending her hat up into the air. When Lizzie and Kathy laughed out loud, the counter on Breezy's clownometer registered their laughs.

"Remind me, would you? How much did I sponsor you for?"

"I seem to remember it was ten-pence per laugh."

Meanwhile, Kathy and Lizzie were still laughing hysterically at Sneezy's exploits, causing the dials on Breezy's clownometer to spin. This was going to bankrupt me — I had to put a stop to it.

"Err, Kathy." I tapped her on the shoulder. "Didn't you say we had to go and see to the thing?" She looked puzzled, but I carried on regardless. "Sorry, Sneezy. Sorry, Breezy, but we have to go and see to the — err — thing."

"No problem, Jill. We should be moving on anyway." Breezy made his bow tie spin around, sending Lizzie once more into hysterics, and no doubt costing me a small fortune.

Once the clowns had left, Kathy took me to one side. "What was that all about, Jill? What is this thing we have to go and see to?"

"Err, nothing. I must have got mixed up."

"You're up to something."

"Me? No, I'm not."

"Can we go now that Auntie Jill is back, Mummy?" Lizzie tugged at her mother's skirt.

"Yes, in a minute."

"Where are you off to?" I asked.

"Show Auntie Jill the flyer, Lizzie."

"I'm going to get a free cuddly clown, Auntie Jill." She handed me a small glossy leaflet.

"Free? Why would they give them away? There must be a catch."

"Why are you always so suspicious?" Kathy rolled her eyes at me. "Look, it says right there that all she has to do is go to the Big Red Clown Tent, present the flyer, and claim her free cuddly clown." She turned to Lizzie. "Mummy has to call at the toilets first."

"Aww, Mummy. All the cuddly clowns will be gone when we get there."

"No, they won't. It says that the tent doesn't open until two o'clock and it's only a quarter past one. Come on, let's go."

"See ya, Auntie Jill!" Lizzie skipped away.

"Bye."

I had bad vibes about this. Very bad vibes.

Why would anyone give away cuddly toys when they could easily sell them? Those flyers were guaranteed to attract children to the Big Red Clown Tent, but what would be waiting for them there? I had a horrible feeling that it might be a wicked witch named Edna Eyesore.

I had to get there before Kathy and Lizzie. Fortunately, they were going via the toilets, but that still didn't leave me much time. I cast the 'faster' spell and sped over there. Once at the tent, I nipped around the back, and cast the 'doppelganger' spell so I would look like Lizzie.

A board outside the front of the tent said that it would open at two, but I had no intention of waiting until then.

"Hello, little girl." The creepy clown greeted me when I stepped into the tent. Even though she was wearing a costume and makeup, I knew it was Edna because I recognised her voice. "You're a little early."

"Sorry," I said in Lizzie's voice.

"That's okay. Is your mummy or daddy with you?"

"No, I'm all by myself. Can I have my cuddly clown?"

"Of course you can." She pointed to a huge pile of them. I had to hand it to Edna, she was smart. Any kid who came into the tent accompanied by their parent would no doubt walk away with a toy. But for any kid who came in unaccompanied, there would be an altogether different surprise.

"What's your name, little girl?"

"Lizzie."

"Well, Lizzie, before you can have your cuddly clown, I need you to come over here, and write your name on this sheet of paper. Can you write your name?"

"Of course I can. I'm a big girl now."

"Okay, then. Come over here."

I took the pen she offered, and I was about to write Lizzie's name when Edna grabbed me from behind. "I've got you now, my little beauty. You're going to make a delicious treacle tart."

"I don't think so, Edna." I reversed the 'doppelganger' spell, and then pushed her away.

"You!"

"You remember me, then?"

"Of course I do. You were the one who got me locked up!" She launched herself at me, but I dodged out of the way, and stuck out a foot. She tripped over it, and went spiralling into the pile of cuddly clowns. Before she had the chance to get up, I used the 'tie-up' spell to bind her hands and feet.

"Get these off! Let me go!"

"Shush!" I magicked a gag over her mouth, to keep her quiet.

Job done. Now all I had to do was find Daze and Blaze, so they could take Edna back to jail in Candlefield.

When I glanced through the flaps of the tent, there was a queue of kids, most of them accompanied by their parents, and at the very head of the queue were Kathy and Lizzie.

Oh bum, bum, bum!

What was I supposed to do now? I could make myself invisible and slip away, but what about the wicked witch clown lying, bound and gagged on the floor? If the kids saw her, they'd be traumatised for life. And if Lizzie didn't get her cuddly clown, she'd be inconsolable. There was only one thing for it.

I rolled Edna over to the cuddly toys, and piled them on top of her, so she was out of sight. Next, I did something really traumatic — I used magic to make myself look like a clown, complete with makeup and stupid costume.

"Hello, children!" I shouted in my best clown voice. "You can come in one at a time."

Kathy and Lizzie were the first into the tent. Lizzies' little eyes almost popped out of her head when she saw the pile of cuddly clowns.

"What's your name, little girl?"

"I'm Lizzie. What's *your* name?"

"Err — I'm — err — "

"Have you forgotten your name?"

"Of course not. It's — err — Peasy. Like Easy Peasy."

"That's a funny name."

"I hope so. I'm a clown — I'm supposed to be funny. Is this your mummy?"

"Yes. She's a bit orange today, but I'm not supposed to talk about it."

Kathy's expression was priceless, and I very nearly lost my — well, you get my drift.

"Go and help yourself to a cuddly clown, Lizzie."

"Thank you, Peasy."

"No problem."

My brilliant plan to hide Edna under the pile of cuddly clowns was beginning to unravel. I hadn't taken into account how many kids would want to claim their free toy. Two hours later, I'd seen hundreds of them. Towards the end, my patience was growing thin, and a few parents looked less than happy when Peasy snapped at their little darlings. That was the least of my problems, though. The pile of cuddly toys had almost disappeared. If many more were claimed, Edna would become visible.

"I'm Brice!" The young boy with a runny nose declared. "This is my mummy."

"Hello, Brice. I'm Peasy." I turned to his mother. "Are there many more waiting outside?"

"No, we're the last ones, I think."

"Help yourself to a cuddly clown, Brice."

He ran over to the small pile of toys and grabbed one.

"There's someone under here, Mummy."

Oh bum!

"I don't think there is, Brice," I said.

"There is. Look! It's another clown."

I had no choice. I cast the 'forget' spell on mother and son, and then led them out of the tent. After putting up a makeshift 'Closed' sign, I went in search of Daze and Blaze. All of the clowns looked the same to me, so it was another twenty minutes before I finally tracked them down.

After leaving them to process Edna, I was finally able to rid myself of the clown persona. I certainly wasn't sorry to see the back of Peasy.

"Where on earth have you been?" Kathy said. "I was beginning to think you'd gone home."

"I've been walking around, taking in all the sights. I see you have your cuddly clown, Lizzie."

"I'm going to call it Peasy, like the clown that gave it to me."

"That's nice."

"Have you noticed anything, Jill?" Kathy said.

I glanced around, but nothing leapt out at me, so I decided to be diplomatic. "Your tan has faded a little?"

"The picnic basket!"

"What about it?"

"It's gone."

"Where?"

"I don't know where. When we got back, it had disappeared, and so had you. I thought you were supposed to be guarding it."

"I didn't think anyone would want to steal a silly picnic basket."

"Pete's parents bought us that *silly picnic basket* for Christmas."

"Oh, sorry."

"I suppose we'd better get going. Pete and Mikey will be back home soon. Pete won't be impressed when I tell him that the picnic basket has been stolen."

"You can blame me if you like."

"Don't worry. I intend to."

***

It was almost nine o'clock when Jack arrived home from his course.

"Hi, you." He greeted me with a kiss.

"How was the course?"

"Tedious beyond belief. How was your picnic?"

"That orange sister of mine got me there under false pretences."

"*Orange?*"

"You should see her. She went to Deli's salon for a spray tan, and it turned her orange. For some reason, she blames me."

"I don't see how it's your fault it went wrong."

"Deli did mention they picked up the equipment on the cheap."

"But you warned Kathy about that, right?"

"It must have slipped my mind."

"In that case, I can see why she might not be best pleased with you. What did you mean when you said Kathy got you there under false pretences?"

"We did go for a picnic in Washbridge Park, but she failed to mention that they were holding the Clownathon there."

"Oh dear. You're not a big fan of clowns, are you?"

"I'm even less of one now, but you haven't heard the half of it."

"I'm gagging for a cup of tea. Why don't I make us both a cuppa, and you can tell me all about it?"

And that's what I did.

"Peasy?" He laughed.

"It was the best I could come up with at short notice. I thought of Sneezy and Breezy, and the name came to me."

"Did Kathy take a photo of Lizzie with Peasy?"

"No, thank goodness."

"That's a pity. I bet you made a sexy clown."

Chapter 15

The giant clown picked me up, and no matter how hard I struggled, I couldn't escape its iron grip. As I got closer and closer to its gaping mouth and those rotten teeth, I was completely helpless.

"Jill!"

I didn't want to die this way; as a snack for some oversized clown.

"Jill! Your phone is ringing!"

"What?" I sat up in bed. "The clown was going to eat me."

"You were dreaming," Jack said. "It's just turned two o'clock. Who's calling you at this hour of the morning?"

I grabbed my phone from the bedside table.

"Is that the woman from the council?" A man's voice said.

"You must have a wrong number."

"Are you sure? Cheesy gave me this number."

"Hold on. Cheesy from the toll bridge?"

"Yeah. He said I had to call you if I saw anyone putting up more graffiti."

"Are you Gordy?" I swung my legs out of bed.

"Yeah. There's someone here now, spraying the bridge."

"Okay. I'll be over there in a few minutes."

"Shall I tell them you're coming?"

"No, don't say anything. I don't want you to scare them off."

"Righto."

"Where are you going?" Jack yawned.

"To catch the person responsible for the graffiti."

"I'll come with you."

"No. You stay in bed. I can handle this."

"Okay, but only if you're sure." He rolled over and was snoring before I had even reached the bedroom door.

I threw on some clothes, jumped in the car, and headed for the toll bridge. Unsurprisingly, the roads at that hour were practically deserted.

I pulled up a hundred yards short of the bridge, and made my way from there on foot. It was dark, but the light from the toll booth revealed a hooded figure stooped next to the wall of the bridge.

"Got you!" I'd managed to sneak up behind them without them hearing.

The hooded figure stood up and turned around to face me.

"Alicia?"

Her face was devoid of expression, and although she was staring directly at me, she registered no sign of recognition.

"Alicia!" I took her by the shoulders and gave her a gentle shake. "Can you hear me?"

"Jill?" For the first time, she seemed to register my presence. "Where am I?" She looked around. "What time is it? What day is it?"

"Let me have this." I took the aerosol can from her hand. "Come with me."

"Where are we going?"

"I'm going to take you home with me."

"Do you think we should call a doctor or take her to A&E?" Jack said.

He'd heard us get back, and had come downstairs to see what was going on. Alicia was resting on the sofa, while Jack and I made a cup of tea.

"Not yet. Let's give her some time to see how she is. She's already showing signs of snapping out of it."

"Out of what, though? What happened to her?"

"I'm not sure, but I'd bet my life that Ma Chivers is behind it."

"That woman sounds like a really nasty piece of work."

"You don't know the half of it. She's never forgiven Alicia for breaking ranks."

Two hours and several cups of tea later, Alicia was looking much better. I'd sent Jack back to bed, so Alicia and I could talk freely.

"Do you think I might have painted the other graffiti?" she said.

"I'm pretty sure you must have."

"I don't remember anything that has happened for the last week or so. I don't even know where I've been." Her voice caught in her throat. "I'm never going to be free of that woman, am I, Jill?"

"Yes, you will. You've done the hard part by breaking away from her."

"I haven't broken away from her, though, have I? Not if she can still control me like this."

"Listen to me. I'm going to put a stop to this, I promise."

"How?"

"I don't know yet, but you're going to stay here until I've figured it out."

"I couldn't impose on you like that."

"Don't be silly. You're staying and that's all there is to it."

"What about your husband? What will you tell him? It must be difficult enough keeping your secret from him without all of this."

"Let me worry about Jack. I'm afraid you'll have to sleep on the sofa, though. The spare bedroom is uninhabitable at the moment."

"That's okay."

"I'm going to go back to bed to see if I can catch a few hours' sleep. Goodnight."

"Goodnight, and Jill, thanks."

"How is she?" Jack was still wide awake when I went upstairs.

"Much better. I've told her she can stay here until I get this sorted out."

"How are you going to do that?"

"I don't have a clue, but I can't let this continue. I'm not doing this just for Alicia. If I don't put a stop to this, it could come back and bite me in the bum. That reminds me, don't forget that Alicia doesn't know that you know I'm a sup."

"That's okay. I'm getting used to people not knowing that I know. Is she still on the sofa?"

"Yeah. I would have given her the spare bedroom, but it's still full of your junk."

"What do you mean, *junk*?"

***

Alicia was still asleep when Jack and I left for work. I

didn't like to disturb her, so I left a note, telling her to make herself at home, but not to go outside under any circumstances.

So far, I'd made precious little headway with either the missing person case, or the murder in Middle Tweaking. I now also had the added complication of Alicia, and how to safeguard her from Ma Chivers.

It promised to be another interesting week.

"Morning, Mrs V."

"Morning, Jill. Did you see any suspicious characters out there?"

"Err, no. Why?"

"If those crocheters can't listen in electronically, I wouldn't put it past them to send spies."

"Is there actually anything here for them to spy on?"

She glanced furtively around, and then took a small black notebook out of her top drawer. Speaking in barely more than a whisper, she said, "These are the plans for our conference. Those crocheters would kill to get their hands on these. Would you like to see them?"

"No, thanks. You'd better put them back in the drawer. Just in case."

"You're right. You can never be too careful."

"If anyone asks, you haven't seen me." Winky's voice came from under the sofa.

I crouched so I could see him. "Who are you hiding from?"

"No one. Just don't tell anyone I'm here."

"If you want me to lie for you, you're going to have to tell me what's going on."

"Bruiser is on the warpath."

"The cat you gave the tattoo? Why's he after you?"

Winky shrugged.

"If you don't tell me, I won't cover for you."

"Okay, okay. There's a bit of a problem with the tattoo I did for him."

"What kind of problem?"

"Apparently, it's become infected."

"That's not necessarily your fault. He may not have kept it clean. Provided that you thoroughly sterilised the equipment before you used it, I don't see that you have anything to worry about. You did sterilise it, didn't you?"

"It seemed like a lot of bother for nothing."

"Oh boy. How bad is the infection?"

"I haven't seen it myself, but from what I hear, there's green pus involved."

"Gross."

***

I had hoped to get hold of Grandma, to discuss the 'Alicia problem', but she wasn't answering her phone, so I decided to take a trip over to Candlefield, to see if Aunt Lucy had any idea where Grandma might be.

"I'm glad you're here, Jill. Barry has been driving me crazy. He keeps asking when you'll be coming over." Just then, there was the unmistakeable sound of huge paws on the stairs. "That sounds like him now."

"Jill!" Barry launched himself at me. "Guess what?"

"You like going for a walk?"

"Yes, I do, but that's not it. I have big news!"

"I'm all ears."

"No, you're not. You have a nose and mouth, too. And eyes."

"No, it's just a saying. Never mind, what's your big news?"

"I've finished my poem."

"The one for Rhymes?"

"Yeah. Do you want to hear it?"

"Of course."

He took a deep breath, and then began to recite.

Rhymes is a tortoise,
Rhymes has a shell,
I like Rhymes,
I liked Hamlet too.

I waited for more, but then I realised he'd finished.

"Do you like it, Jill?"

"Yeah, it's—err—very nice. Has Rhymes heard it yet?"

"No, I wanted you to hear it first, to make sure it was okay."

"I think it's very good for a first attempt."

"Thanks, Jill. I hope Rhymes likes it too." He shot out of the door and back upstairs.

Aunt Lucy and I looked at one another.

"It almost rhymed," she said.

"I'm sure Rhymes will love it."

"I do hope so or Barry will be devastated. Would you like a cup of tea?"

"No, thanks. I wondered if you had any idea where Grandma is? She isn't answering her phone."

"She's gone on a day trip with WOW."

"Wow?"

"The Witches of Washbridge."

"Oh yes, I remember now. She told me about them some time ago. Isn't she the chair?"

"She is indeed."

"I still haven't had my invitation to join them yet."

"Do you want one?"

"Not really."

"It's their annual day trip to the seaside. They've gone to Candle Sands, and won't be back until late. Was it urgent?"

"Kind of, but it can wait one day. While I'm here, do you happen to know where I can find the Sinkhole Tavern."

"You mustn't go there." She looked horrified. "It's a ghastly place with a terrible reputation."

"I have no choice. There's someone I need to speak to, and that's where he hangs out, apparently."

"Anyone who frequents that place is bad news. Please be careful."

"I always am."

"Do you know the sewage works?"

"Surprisingly enough, no." I laughed. "It's not somewhere I've ever had the urge to visit."

"I suppose not. It's due South from here — you'll know when you're getting close."

"How?"

She raised her eyebrows at my stupidity.

"Right, sorry. And the tavern is close by, is it?"

"Practically next door."

"Wish me luck, then."

***

Oh boy! What an awful smell.

Why would anyone in their right mind build a tavern next door to a sewage works? But then, judging by the state of the tavern, I guessed it had probably been there first. Either way, you had to wonder why anyone would choose to drink there. Other than the tavern and sewage works, there were no other buildings in sight.

"You can't come in here." The wizard barring my way was so ugly it should have been a criminal offence.

"Why not?"

"No women allowed in here. It's men only in the Sinkhole Tavern."

"You can't bar people based on their gender."

"Says who?"

"Says the law."

He laughed. "The law don't apply around these parts."

Although I was appalled at the blatant sexism, I was even more shocked that they could afford to turn away custom. Judging by what I could see over Ugly's shoulder, the tavern looked to be pretty much empty.

"I'm looking for someone."

"Aren't we all, love? You should try a dating agency."

"I'm looking for someone in particular. Columbus Dark, do you know him?"

He shrugged.

"I have it under good authority that he frequents this — err — establishment."

"Makes no odds either way. You can't come in."

"Okay, let me make this very simple for you. Either you let me in, or I turn you into a cockroach."

"You?" He laughed. "That I'd like to see."

I was about to oblige when from somewhere inside the

tavern a voice boomed, "Let her in, Grainger!"

Ugly turned around. "Let her in?"

"You heard me."

"But she's a woman."

"I can see that. Move out of the way, and let the young lady through the door. Don't make me say it again."

Ugly turned back to me, scowled, but then stepped to one side.

"Thank you, Grainger." I flashed him a smile on my way past.

It took a few seconds for my eyes to adjust to the dark. As I'd suspected, the place was practically deserted. Apart from the wizard behind the bar, there were only three customers. One of whom beckoned to me.

"I believe you're looking for me?"

"Are you Columbus Dark?"

"At your service. I must apologise for Grainger. He has the manners of a pig."

"Why don't they allow women in here?"

"They never have, but to be honest, it's not really a problem. There aren't many women who would want to come to the Sinkhole. Or men, for that matter."

"So why do *you* come here?"

"I was a customer here before the sewage works were built, and the habit kind of stuck. And besides, they still serve the best ale in Candlefield."

"They must do."

"I've rarely encountered a witch with as much spirit as you just demonstrated. There was one, but that was many moons ago now."

"Her name wouldn't happen to be Mirabel, would it?"

"How did you know?"

"Mirabel Millbright is my grandmother. She mentioned that you and she were once an item."

"Well, well." He chuckled. "That explains everything. The apple certainly didn't fall far from the tree with you, did it? How is Mirabel?"

"As cantankerous as ever."

"That's my Mirabel. I could tell you stories about your grandmother that would make you blush."

"Probably better you don't."

"You may be right." He laughed. "Still, happy memories. No wonder you weren't scared of Grainger. If the stories I've heard are true, you're one of the most powerful witches Candlefield has ever known. Why are you looking for old Columbus?"

"I wanted to talk to you about world generators?"

"In that case, it's a pity you didn't come and see me two hundred years ago. I've been out of that business for over a century."

"That's funny because I heard you'd sold one recently."

His face fell. "I knew that was a mistake. What's happened?"

"You admit you sold it, then?"

"Only because they wouldn't take no for an answer. It was an old one I've had kicking around for ages, but it needs repairing. I explained all of this to them, but they insisted they wanted it anyway. Has something bad happened?"

"Two humans have become trapped inside it."

"Those stupid idiots. They should never have allowed humans anywhere near it."

"Can you repair it and get them out?"

"Not without a blue star crystal, and they're rarer than

hen's teeth. That's why I haven't repaired it before now."

"If you had the crystal, would you be able to mend the thing, and get the humans out?"

"Yeah, easy, but there's a shortage of crystals, and they cost a small fortune."

"What if I could get one for you?"

He laughed. "I know you're a powerful witch, but even you can't produce a blue star crystal using magic. How are you going to get one?"

"I'm going to call in a favour. Stay right there. I'll be back."

What do you mean someone else has already claimed that catchphrase?

Chapter 16

This was going to be tricky. If I didn't get the co-ordinates just right, I could be in for a very rough landing. But I had no choice, it had to be done.

"Kip, kip, kip!"

"Sorry, Cora, I didn't mean to land in your nest."

"Kip, kip, kip!"

"Ouch. Don't do that." I scrambled out before she could nip me again with her baby dragon teeth.

Moments later, a shadow fell over me, and I heard the sound of huge dragon wings.

"Jill?" Sybil put down next to me. "I heard Cora crying and thought those funny little elf creatures were back."

"It's just me. Sorry, I got my coordinates slightly wrong—I didn't intend to land in her nest."

"How did you get up here? I didn't see you on the mountainside."

"I cheated and used magic."

"Why have you come back? Is everything okay?"

"Yeah. Actually, I was hoping to ask you a small favour."

"If it's about the flying creature—what did you call it? The airship? It's flown past a few times since you were last here, and as I promised, I didn't chase it away."

"Thanks, I'm really grateful, but actually, I was hoping you might be able to take me to the village where the elves live. It would take me forever to find it by myself."

"I'll be happy to. Climb on my back and we'll be there in no time."

You might think that flying on a dragon's back is cool, but let me tell you, it really isn't—it's very scary. I had to hold on for dear life, as Sybil swooped down from the mountain towards the forest below.

"Do you see the clearing over there, Jill?"

"Yeah."

"That's where the funny little creatures live. You'd better be ready to jump off because I don't think they'll be very happy to see me."

"Okay."

As we made our final approach, I could see the elves below me. They were all diving for cover into their small wooden houses. Once we were on the ground, I slid down Sybil's tail, and then waved goodbye, as she headed back to her nest.

There were still no elves in sight, but I heard someone shout, "Jill? Is that you?"

"Cyrus? Where are you?"

"Over here." He poked his head out from one of the small houses. "Has the dragon gone?"

"Yeah, it's perfectly safe now. I asked her to bring me to your village."

He edged slowly out of the house, whilst checking the sky to make sure Sybil wasn't still around.

"What brings you back here, Jill?"

"I was hoping I might be able to call in that favour."

"Of course. What can we do for you?"

"I need a blue star crystal if that's possible."

"No problem. What size do you want?"

"Size? Err, I'm not really sure."

"What's it for?"

I told Cyrus all about the faulty world generator, and

how I was trying to rescue two humans trapped inside it.

"If it's for a world generator, you need a size three crystal."

"Is that big? Will I be able to carry it?"

"I think you'll manage." He laughed. "Wait there and I'll get one for you."

While I waited, more elves ventured out of their houses. After a while, I began to feel a little self-conscious, as they stared at me, and talked in hushed voices.

"There you are." Cyrus held out his open palm.

"Is that it?" I picked up the tiny crystal, which was no bigger than the stone in my engagement ring.

"Yeah. Size three."

"Thanks very much."

"My pleasure. Will you stay and have something to eat with us? We don't normally get visitors out here."

"That's very kind of you, but I need to get back, so I can rescue the humans."

"Will the dragon be coming back for you?" He glanced up at the sky.

"No, it's okay. I have a much quicker way of getting back."

***

"One blue star crystal as requested." I held it between my thumb and index finger. "Size three."

"Well, I never." Columbus spilled a little of his beer. "And it's top quality too. Not like the ones I usually have to settle for. Where on earth did you get that?"

"I'll explain later. Right now, I need you to make good on your promise to repair the world generator, so we can get the two trapped humans back."

"Columbus Dark is a man of his word." He downed the beer in one go. "Lead the way, young lady."

We magicked ourselves to Washbridge, but my timing couldn't have been worse because Mrs V came out of the office when Columbus and I were halfway up the stairs.

"Jill are you alright?" She was staring at the shady looking character standing next to me.

"I'm fine, Mrs V. This is—err—"

"Columbus Dark, at your service." He bowed. "Is this your coven?"

Oh boy!

"Coven?" Mrs V looked puzzled. "What do you mean?"

"He didn't say *coven*." I jumped in quickly. "He said *oven*. Columbus is here to mend my oven."

"What oven?"

"My—err—microwave oven. It's in the car."

"So why is he in here?"

"I left my car keys in my drawer."

"I see. Well, I'd better get a move on. I have a dentist appointment in ten minutes."

"Oh?"

"I did mention it last week, Jill."

"Yes, of course. I remember now."

Columbus moved to one side to allow her to pass. As she did, she eyed him suspiciously. "Are you sure you'll be okay, Jill?"

"Yes, I'm fine, thanks."

"What a handsome lady," Columbus said, after Mrs V had left the building. "I think she may have taken a shine to me."

"Never mind Mrs V. You have work to do."

Lucas and Wendy were surprised to see me, but even more surprised to see Columbus.

"I warned you two that the generator wasn't firing on all cylinders." He scolded them. "What were you thinking?"

"We're really sorry," Lucas said.

Wendy said nothing.

"Where is it?" Columbus demanded.

"This way." Lucas opened the door behind him. "It's in here."

"I'm going to leave you to it, Columbus," I said. "I'll be in my office, just down the corridor. Will you come and let me know as soon as you've rescued the young couple?"

"I will. It shouldn't take long now that I have the crystal."

***

There was a cat in the outer office, but it wasn't Winky.

"Where is he?" Bruiser demanded.

"Who?"

"You know very well who. Winky!"

"What do you want with him?"

"Just a quiet word about this." He pulled back his fur patch to reveal the tattoo, which was oozing with green pus.

"Yuk! Put that away."

"Now you can see why I'd like a few words with my dear friend, Winky."

"He's gone away for a few days, err—weeks. Probably

months."

"Gone away where?"

"To his brother's."

"I don't believe you." Bruiser started for my office, and before I could stop him, he was through the door.

I had to act quickly.

"I know he's in here somewhere." Bruiser rushed around the office. "Where is he?"

"I've already told you. He's gone to stay with his brother, and I don't know when or even if he'll be coming back."

He ran over to the sofa and peered underneath it. "Someone must have tipped him off that I was looking for him."

"Can I pass on a message if I hear from Winky?"

"Tell him that his days are numbered." And with that threat, Bruiser left.

"Has he gone?" Winky called from under the sofa.

"Yes, you can come out now."

"I thought I was a goner there."

"You would have been if I hadn't used magic to hide you."

"Thanks. You're a diamond. Haven't I always said so?"

***

When Columbus eventually came through to my office, he was accompanied by two very confused young people.

"You must be Mark and Susan." I walked over to greet them.

"What day is it?" Susan looked and sounded

disorientated.

"What's going on?" Mark said.

"There's nothing to worry about," I reassured them. "Everything's okay now."

"But you don't understand. Susan and I have been stuck in that escape room for days. It was like a maze with no exit."

"You're out now. That's all that matters."

"Who are you two, anyway?" Mark said. "Do you work at the escape room?"

They were asking way too many questions, and although that was perfectly understandable, I couldn't provide them with an answer that would have made a lick of sense.

Ignoring Mark's question, I turned to Columbus. "Thanks for your help. I can take this from here."

"I thought I might hang around until your friend comes back."

"I don't think that's a very good idea. Mrs V is already spoken for. Can you make your own way back?"

"Of course, but please tell Mrs V to give me a call if she ever needs company."

"I'll be sure to do that."

He then vanished into thin air, leaving poor old Mark and Susan even more confused.

"He just disappeared!" Susan said. "Where did he go?"

"He's just nipped out."

"But one minute he was standing there, and the next—"

"You both look shattered. Why don't you sit down and rest for a few minutes?"

As soon as they were seated, I cast the 'sleep' spell on both of them.

It would require some pretty nifty magic to make them forget their awful ordeal in the escape room. I also had to come up with a plausible explanation as to where they'd been for the last few days.

But, as always, I had a plan.

First stop: Candle Sands.

Once I'd magicked myself there, it wasn't difficult to track down Grandma and the other WOW members. I just followed the sound of cackling.

"What are you doing here?" Grandma was obviously delighted to see me. "This is a WOW outing. Members only."

"Don't worry; I'm not staying. I need your advice, please."

"Couldn't it have waited until I got back?"

"Actually, no. It'll only take a minute, I promise."

"It had better. We were about to go and get candyfloss."

I explained that we'd rescued the young couple from the escape room, and that now I needed to find a way of making them forget their awful experience.

"You found Columbus, then?"

"Yes. He remembered you."

"Of course he did."

"What do you think I should do, Grandma?"

"I would have thought that would be obvious to the *most powerful witch in Candlefield.*" Only she could say that and make it sound like an insult.

"Well, it isn't obvious to me."

"You'll need to implant an alternate memory."

"Like what?"

"I don't know. Use your imagination. What else could

they have been up to for the last few days?"

"It was his birthday, so I suppose they might have gone away somewhere."

"Bingo! Now, can I go and get my candyfloss?"

"Wait! There's something else I need to talk to you about."

"It'll have to wait."

"It's about Ma Chivers."

"I said it will have to wait. Right now, I need candyfloss."

"Okay, thanks for your help."

An implanted memory! Now she'd said it, it was so obvious, so why hadn't I thought of it?

Next stop: London.

After using the 'doppelganger' spell to make myself look like Mark Blythe, I booked into a budget hotel in North London.

Final stop: Back to the office.

"What is going on, Jill?"

Oh bum! Mrs V was back from the dentist.

"What do you mean?"

"When I got back, I found these two young people in here, fast asleep."

"Err, they're Kathy's friends. They've come to visit."

"But why are they asleep?"

"They've had a long journey. Look, why don't you call it a day, Mrs V?"

"But it isn't time for me to finish yet."

"I know, but if you're working at your desk, you might wake them up, and they need their rest."

"I do have a lot of work to do for the conference."

"It's decided, then. Off you trot."

"Okay, dear. I'll see you tomorrow."

"Bye, Mrs V."

Using magic to transport two people isn't easy at the best of times. Doing it while they're fast asleep, and trying to ensure we ended up in the correct hotel room, was a challenge and a half.

But, of course, this superstar witch managed it.

After implanting memories from a day trip I'd taken to London when I was a kid, I left them dozing on the double bed.

Back at the office, I called Susan's father.

"Mr Longacre, it's Jill Maxwell."

"Jill? Do you have any news for us?"

"I do. I've managed to locate them, and they're both safe and sound."

"Thank goodness for that. Where are they?"

"In a hotel in London."

"I don't understand. Why on earth didn't they tell us that's where they were going? And why haven't they been answering their phones?"

"That's young people for you, I'm afraid. Too caught up in their own lives to worry about anyone else."

"It's not like them. Either of them. Still, they're alright, and that's all that matters."

"I'll text you details of the hotel and room number where they're staying."

"Thank you so much for your help. I'll have a few words to say to both of them, for worrying us like this."

"Don't be too hard on them. You're only young once."

I felt a little guilty at having to paint the young couple in a bad light when in fact they'd done nothing wrong, but what choice did I have?

Chapter 17

I felt terrible about Myrtle. There she was, languishing in prison, and so far, I'd made precious little progress in finding the real murderer. And it wasn't as though I could tell her why I appeared to be dragging my feet.

"Sorry, Myrtle, but I had to stop a dragon attacking an airship, and then I had to collect a crystal from some elves, so I could free a couple trapped inside a 'world generator' spell."

She would probably think I'd been eating funny mushrooms.

At least now that I'd put the missing person case to bed, I could give my full attention to the Middle Tweaking murder. My first port of call would be The Old Trout public house. Except that it was no longer The Old Trout; the pub was now called The Boomerang.

Inside, it was almost unrecognisable from my previous visit. The furniture had all been replaced, and there was no sign of the fishing trophies or photographs that had once filled the place. Instead, on every wall, hung dozens of boomerangs.

The pub had only just opened for the day, and I appeared to be their first customer.

"Welcome to The Boomerang." The man behind the bar was wearing a tie with little boomerangs on it. "What can I get for you?"

"A lime and soda, please."

"Coming right up. Ice?"

"Yes, please. The last time I was in here, it was called The Old Trout."

"Some of the locals still wish it was." He smiled. "I'm

afraid that not everyone approves of the change of name."

"I kind of like it. Are you the owner?"

"Yes, I'm Ronnie. My wife and I bought the place just over a year ago. The last person to own the pub left under rather unfortunate circumstances."

"The murder of the postmistress, you mean?"

"That's right. Are you a local, then? I haven't seen you around the village before."

"No, but I worked with Myrtle Turtle on the Madge Hick case."

"We foolishly thought the locals would be happy to see the old name disappear, given what had happened."

"Aren't they?"

"Most of them are okay with it, but a few still insist on calling it by its old name." He grinned. "It hasn't stopped any of them from drinking here, though."

"Hi, I'm Bonnie." A woman joined him behind the bar. "I'm Ronnie's wife."

"Nice to meet you. I'm Jill. Neither of you has an Australian accent as far as I can make out."

"Why would you expect us to have one?"

"It's just that I saw the boomerangs, and kind of assumed you must be from down under."

"I'm from Cornwall, and Ronnie is from Wimbledon. We both compete in boomerang tournaments. In fact, that's where we first met."

"I had no idea there were tournaments for boomerangs."

"You'd be surprised. They were quite popular some years ago, but then interest seemed to wane for a while, but now the sport is booming again."

"It sounds as though the boomerang has made a bit of a

comeback." I laughed.

Which was just as well, because neither Ronnie nor Bonnie did; they obviously didn't think boomerangs were a suitable subject for levity.

"The reason I'm here today is that I've been asked to help Myrtle Turtle. You know she's been charged with murder, I assume?"

"It's hard to believe Myrtle would do such a thing," Ronnie said. "She can be a bit cantankerous at times — she's one of the regulars who'll probably always call this place The Old Trout — but a murderer? Never."

"She did have a go at Rob that day," Bonnie said. "You saw how angry she was."

"I know, but even so."

"Would you mind talking me through what happened?" I said.

It was Bonnie who began to tell the story. "We've had a few problems with Rob Evans and that skanky girlfriend of his."

"Bonnie!" Ronnie admonished her.

"Sorry, but it's true. The pair of them were as bad as one another. His friends too."

"Are his friends local?"

"No. As far as I can make out, they come up from London. That's where Evans was living before he inherited his grandmother's place. This is normally a quiet village pub, but whenever that lot show up, things almost always get out of hand. We've had to ask them to leave on a couple of occasions."

"Were there many of them in that day?"

"No, it was just Rob, but it was lunchtime, so Sydney was probably still sleeping it off from the night before."

"*Sydney*? Who's he?"

"*She* is Rob's girlfriend. Anyway, it wasn't long before he started to get louder and louder; he was shouting at everyone about nothing in particular. I was about to tell Ronnie to throw him out when Myrtle stepped in. She usually comes in with those two strange friends of hers."

"Hodd and Jobbs?"

"Yes, but that day she was having a quiet drink by herself. Anyway, Myrtle started to lay into Rob. She told him a few home truths—not that it did any good. They had a stand-up slanging match right there in the middle of the floor. In the end, Rob backed down and stormed out. He wasn't happy."

"Did he threaten her?"

"Not that I heard."

"What did Myrtle do after he'd left?"

"She apologised to everyone for the commotion, and then went back to her drink. The next thing we heard was the following day when someone told us that Rob's body had been found in the river. We assumed he'd fallen in, but then they arrested Myrtle."

"Had you ever heard anyone else threaten Rob?"

"He didn't have many friends in the village. A lot of people said they'd be glad to see the back of him, but I wouldn't say anyone actually threatened him."

"Any strangers in the village recently?"

"Only Rob's London friends."

"Okay, thanks for your help." I drained the last of my lime and soda.

"No problem," Ronnie said. "If there's anything else you need, give us a shout. We hate to think of poor Myrtle in prison."

"I don't suppose you have any idea where I might find Rob's girlfriend, do you?"

"As far as I know, she's been staying in Rob's house since he died."

***

Before I could go and see Sydney, I had some other extremely important business to attend to.

"And a blueberry muffin, please."

"Coming right up, Jill," Mindy said.

What do you mean, *what happened to giving my full attention to the murder case*? How can I be expected to function effectively if I have a blueberry deficiency? And besides, I hadn't been in Cuppy C for ages.

"I assume the twins are out somewhere, enjoying their family day, are they?"

Amber and Pearl had persuaded their husbands, Alan and William, to change their shifts, so that they would all be off together on Mondays.

"Actually, the twins are upstairs." Mindy handed me the muffin.

"What happened to 'Monday is family day'?"

"Between you and me, Jill, I think that was a ruse to get Alan and William to look after the kids on Mondays, so the twins could do their thing."

"What are they doing upstairs?"

"I'm not sure. I think they have some kind of new plan for this place."

"Oh dear. I'd better go and see what they're up to."

"Hello, you two. I thought Monday was supposed to be

family day."

"Sorry?" Amber put her hand to her ear. "I can't hear you for that muffin in your mouth."

"Very funny. Mindy tells me you two are planning something up here."

"This is our best idea ever," Pearl gushed.

"Ever! Ever!" Amber was every bit as enthusiastic as her sister.

"You do realise you've said this before. Many times."

"This is different, and it all stems from our being new mums."

"Go on, then. Impress me."

"We're going to open a creche."

"Up here?"

"Yes. These rooms are just standing empty. We'll get these walls knocked out to create one large space. Mums will be able to come up here with their kids, and we'll be able to sell them drinks and snacks."

"I'm worried."

"What is it this time, Jill?" Amber snapped. "You're always such a downer."

"I'm worried because it actually sounds like a sensible plan."

"It does?" Pearl was obviously shocked by my reaction.

So too was Amber.

"Yeah, there's just one thing. You said it would be for mums, but surely it will be for dads too."

"You know so little about parenting, Jill." Amber scoffed. "It's always the mums who end up looking after the kids."

"Really? Remind me, where are Lil and Lily?"

***

The young woman who answered the door oozed sophistication. Her makeup (the previous day's, I assumed) had run, and her hair looked as though she'd been hanging upside down for several hours.

"Who are you?" She said through a mouthful of chewing gum.

"My name is Jill Maxwell."

"If you're looking for Rob, he's dead. Murdered."

"Actually, it was you I wanted to speak to. I assume you're Sydney?"

"If it's about my living here, I—"

"It isn't. Could we talk inside?"

"I suppose so." She spat out the gum, and then took out a pack of cigarettes and lit one.

The house must have been beautiful. Once. But not now. It bore the scars from a dozen wild parties. The carpets were all stained, the sofa was torn and covered in cigarette burns, and the whole place reeked of booze and drugs. The only saving grace was that Rob's grandmother wasn't still alive to see what had become of her home.

"What do you want?" Sydney took a long drag on her cigarette. "I have to nip down the shops in a minute."

"I'm a private investigator."

"Really? Cool. I wouldn't mind a job like that. Do you need qualifications and stuff?"

"Some, yeah. Can you tell me about the day Rob died?"

"I don't know anything."

"I understand he was in The Boomerang at lunchtime."

"So I heard."

"Why weren't you with him?"

"I was stuck at home by myself. I couldn't get in touch with him because I'd lost my phone."

"So, you were here? In this house?"

"No, I just told you. I was at home."

"Back in London?"

"Jeez, how did you ever get to be a private investigator? I was at home in Little Bigging. It's about eight miles up the road from here."

"Sorry. I thought you and Rob had moved here together from London."

"Nah, I didn't know him until a couple of months ago. Me and a few friends heard about his parties, so we gatecrashed one. Rob and I got together after that."

"But you didn't move in with him?"

"I stayed over some nights, but Rob said we should wait a bit before I moved my stuff in."

"I see. If you couldn't phone him, why didn't you come over to Middle Tweaking to see him?"

"I didn't know if he'd be here. He'd said he might go back to London for a few days, to see his mum."

Sydney stubbed out her cigarette. "Are we done, yet? I need to go and get some more ciggies."

"Yeah, we're done, thanks."

As I made my way back to the car, I thought about what Sydney had told me. I wasn't totally convinced by the lost phone story.

***

We were running low on custard creams, so on my way home, I called in at The Corner Shop. I was a little nervous about seeing Little Jack Corner because of the part I'd played in destroying his chances of winning his way through the heats of the annual Corner Shop Stacking Competition. Still, for the sake of my custard cream stash, I would have to face the music.

"Hi, Jill." He greeted me with a smile.

"Hello, Jack. I want to apologise for the other day."

"What do you mean?"

"The stacking competition. I'm sorry that I ruined —"

"I'm through to the finals." He was obviously bursting with pride.

"You are? I thought the cat had knocked them all over."

"He did, but that's what got me through to the final."

"I don't follow."

"My original efforts were all too safe. I would never have got through with that pathetic offering."

"It looked pretty impressive to me."

"To the untrained eye, maybe, but not to the professionals."

"What happened? Did you rebuild them all?"

"I did."

"That must have taken ages."

"I was up all night, but it was well worth it."

"I'm delighted for you. I thought you might have skinned that cat."

"Sooty? No, in fact, I've decided to adopt him. At least until someone claims him."

"What about your other cat?"

"Ginger came back later the same day. The two of them are firm friends now."

"That's great."

"And it's you I have to thank for my success, Jill. If you

hadn't come in when you did, I would probably have been eliminated."

"Shucks, I didn't do anything."

What do you mean, no one says *shucks*? I do, so suck it up.

"I feel like I should give you something to show my gratitude." Little Jack lifted a large box onto the counter. On the side of it were the words: this box contains 60 packets of custard creams.

"That's very kind, but it really isn't necessary."

I was about to grab the huge box when Jack tore it open, took out a single packet, and handed it to me.

"There you go, Jill. Thanks again."

What a cheapskate!

Chapter 18

When I got up the next morning, Alicia was in the kitchen.

"Have you seen Jack?" I yawned.

"He said to tell you that he'd had a call, asking him to go into work early."

"I wonder why he didn't wake me."

"He said he'd tried to, but that you were dead to the world." She grinned. "Snoring your head off, he said."

"Rubbish, I never snore."

"Would you like a cup of tea, Jill? I've only just brewed this."

"That would be great, thanks."

"I think it's time I moved out. It isn't right, imposing myself on you and Jack like this." She poured the tea. "Milk and sugar?"

"Milk and one and two-thirds spoons of sugar, please."

She added the milk, but then passed me my cup of tea and the sugar bowl. "You'd better put your own sugar in. I never was any good at maths."

"You can't leave yet. Not until I make sure that Ma Chivers can't get to you again."

"How are you going to do that?"

"It's all in hand," I lied. "With a bit of luck, it'll all be sorted by the end of the day. Promise me that you won't go outside before then."

"Okay, I promise."

***

Mrs V was knitting a pair of orange socks. Perhaps they

were for Kathy.

"Morning, Mrs V."

"Hmm." She gave me a disapproving look.

"What's wrong?"

"Do you remember the young couple who were fast asleep in here yesterday?"

"Of course. Kathy's friends."

"That's what you told me, yes." She put down her knitting. "Kathy called a few minutes ago. She'd tried to get you on your mobile, but you didn't answer."

"It must have been while I was driving; I didn't hear it." I took the phone out of my pocket, and sure enough there were two missed calls from her. "What did she want?"

"She didn't say; just that she'd like you to call her back."

"Okay, will do."

"I asked her how her friends were today. She had no idea what I was talking about."

"Ah, I can see why you might find that confusing."

"I'm not the one who's confused here, Jill. You definitely told me they were Kathy's friends."

"And so they are. Just not *that* Kathy."

"There's another one?"

"Yeah. My friend, Kathy. Kathy — err — Batty."

"Kathy Batty?"

"Yeah. I'm sure I've mentioned her before."

"I'm certain you haven't."

"Well, anyway, the sleepy couple who were in here yesterday are her friends. Sorry for the confusion. I'd better go and call Kathy now."

"Make sure you call the right one."

"Winky? Why are you wearing a false moustache and

glasses?"

"In case Bruiser comes looking for me again."

"Don't you think he might still recognise you?"

"No chance. I'm the master of disguise."

"O−kay." To escape the insanity of my office, even if only for a few minutes, I called Kathy back.

"Jill! I need you to come straight down here."

"Why? What's up?"

"There's a mouse in the shop. You know I'm scared of them."

"Why are you telling me? I'm scared of them too."

"No, you're not. Not since you had the hypnotherapy."

I was hoping she'd forgotten about that. A few years before, I'd also had a phobia about the silly little rodents, which didn't look good for someone who was supposed to be a tough private investigator. So, despite my reservations, I underwent a short course of hypnotherapy, which to my amazement had actually worked.

"Can't you ask May to put it outside?"

"I would, but she hasn't turned in."

"Is she ill?"

"I don't know. She hasn't called. I'm beginning to think you may have been right about her. Will you come down?"

"I'm really busy, working on a murder case."

"Please, Jill! It'll only take you a few minutes."

"Okay, keep your wig on. I'm on my way."

"There you go again, letting people take advantage of you," said the cat with the glasses and moustache, who looked nothing like Winky. "You need to learn to say no."

"Kathy's scared of mice."

"What a wuss."

"That's pretty rich coming from you. I seem to remember you were terrified of a toy mouse."

"Don't be ridiculous. You must be thinking of someone else."

"Sorry, my bad. I got you mixed up with Winky. You haven't seen him anywhere, have you?"

***

When I arrived at the shop, Kathy was standing on a chair.

"Thank goodness you're here."

"That's the nicest greeting I've had from you in a long time. Where is this monster?"

"It went into the changing room."

"Why are you still standing on the chair, then?"

"It might run out again when you go inside."

"And do what? Tear you limb from limb?"

"Just get rid of it, Jill, will you?"

"Okay. Stay there."

"Don't worry. I don't plan on moving."

I opened the door, just wide enough to squeeze inside, and then closed it behind me.

Right, mousey, where are you?

There was no sign of it. Perhaps there was a hole in the wall somewhere. I got down on all fours, to take a closer look.

"Jill!" The squeaky little voice seemed to come from behind the waste paper basket. "Jill, it's me!"

I moved the basket to one side, to reveal the tiniest grey mouse. I was about to pick it up when it said, "It's me, Jill. May Knott."

"May? You're a mouse."

"I know that."

"Sorry, of course you do. How did it happen?"

"I don't know. Kathy must have been in the back when I arrived. I'd no sooner walked through the door than your grandmother came nosing around. I was about to ask her to leave when everything went kind of fuzzy. When I came around, I was a mouse. I hid in here because I was scared Kathy would squish me."

"Jill!" Kathy shouted from the other room. "Have you found it?"

"Not yet. I'm still looking."

"Hurry up. I'm getting vertigo on this chair."

"Listen, May, I'm going to have to pick you up, and carry you out of the shop."

"What if you drop me?"

"I won't, as long as you don't struggle."

"What's going to happen then? I don't want to be a mouse forever."

"You won't, I promise, but first things first. Stay still while I pick you up."

"Have you caught it?" Kathy was still on the chair when I came out of the changing room.

"Yes." I showed her the mouse in my cupped hands. "I'll take it outside."

"Make sure you drop it off a long way from here or it'll just come back."

"Okay."

After finding a deserted alleyway, I put May on the ground, and then reversed the spell that had turned her into a mouse.

"Thank goodness!" She hugged me. "But what

happened? How could I have been a mouse?"

After casting the 'forget' spell, and while she was still a little disorientated, I led May back onto the high street. "Shouldn't you be at the shop by now, May?"

"Sorry?" She checked her watch. "Goodness, I'm late."

"I'm sure if you explain to Kathy that the bus let you down, she'll understand."

"The bus?"

"It was running late, wasn't it?"

"Err, yeah, I guess it must have been."

***

I'd been hammering on the locked door of Ever for ages before Grandma finally showed her face.

"What's all the noise about? We're not open yet."

"You and I need to talk. Can I come in?"

"Will you go away if I say no?"

"No."

"That's what I thought. You'd better come through to the office, then."

Grandma sat at her desk and took a sip from a cup of steaming green liquid.

"What on earth is that?" The smell was making me feel quite ill.

"It's my patented morning pick-me-up. Would you like a taste?"

"No, thanks. It smells awful."

"It's a lot better for you than that coffee you're always drinking."

"I seriously doubt that."

"Are you going to tell me why you're here, or do I have

to guess?"

"I have a bone to pick with you."

"And here was I thinking you'd come over to shoot the breeze."

"How dare you turn May into a mouse?"

"Who?"

"You know who. Kathy's assistant."

"She was getting on my nerves—the jumped-up little madam."

"She was only acting on Kathy's orders, to keep you out of the shop."

"She was very rude to me."

"That doesn't give you the right to turn her into a mouse."

"Let me guess, you've reversed my spell."

"Of course I have."

"Spoilsport." Grandma took a long drink of the green stuff. "Is that all you wanted?"

"No, actually. I need your help with something."

"Really?" She cackled. "You have a go at me and then expect me to help you?"

"Essentially, yes."

"Go on, then. I'm listening."

"Ma Chivers is at it again."

"What's she done to you this time?"

"She had someone put up graffiti all around Washbridge, saying I was a witch."

"Is that all? You don't need my help to get rid of a bit of graffiti."

"It's not that. I've already had the graffiti removed."

"What is it, then?"

"She made someone do it against their will. I want you

to help me to protect this person from Ma Chivers."

"Who is it?"

"Alicia."

"Are you serious? Have you forgotten that she once tried to kill you?"

"Of course I haven't, but she was under Ma Chivers' influence back then. Alicia has turned over a new leaf and is trying to make a fresh start."

"I never realised how gullible you are."

"I believe her."

"More fool you."

"Will you help me or not?"

"I'd need something in return."

"Don't you always? What is it this time?"

"It's the Elite Competition soon."

"And you want me to be your assistant again? Okay, I'll do it."

"Actually, I've retired from all competitions."

"Since when? Why?"

"I've been at the top for long enough. It's time for me to step aside and give someone else a chance."

"You surely don't mean me, do you?"

"Who else?"

"I can't take part in the Elite Competition—it's for level six witches only. In case you've forgotten, I'm still on level four."

"Which is plainly nonsense. The only reason you're still on level four is because you snubbed the offer to become the first level seven witch."

"I've explained my reasons for that."

"Yes, yes, we don't need to go over that again, but I've checked with the organisers, and as far as they're concerned, you're welcome to participate."

"Why would you do that without asking me first?"

"What's the problem?"

"I have no interest in taking part in that or any other competition."

"Please yourself, but that's my condition for helping you with Alicia."

"That isn't fair."

"Cry me a river."

Although I was now powerful enough to cast almost any spell I wanted, I still didn't have the depth of knowledge or experience that Grandma possessed. Trying to figure out how to foil Ma Chivers' control over Alicia wasn't something I could do alone, but if I wanted Grandma's help, I had no choice but to agree to her terms.

"Let's say I agreed, will you help me?"

"With Alicia? Yes, I've just said so, haven't I?"

"No, I meant with the competition?"

"Of course. You'll need my help if you're going to overcome your main opponent."

"Who's that?"

"Who do you think? Ma Chivers of course."

"Okay, I'll take part in the Elite Competition. Now, can we talk about Alicia?"

Grandma listened in silence as I explained the problems that Alicia had encountered since she'd broken away from Ma Chivers.

"I thought you might be able to come up with some kind of potion to protect her."

"I could, but that would be like putting a sticking plaster over the problem."

"What do you suggest, then?"

"Ma Chivers has to be taken down a peg or two. She draws most of her power from the followers she attracts. If they were all to desert her, she'd be a spent force."

"How are we going to do that?"

"*We* aren't going to do it. *You're* going to do it."

"*Me*? How?"

"In the Elite Competition of course. It won't be enough that you just win it. You have to totally humiliate her in front of all her peers."

"That's easier said than done. If I remember correctly, you only just beat her the last time you competed."

"I never said it was going to be easy."

"In the meantime, what about Alicia?"

"I'll concoct a potion which will hide her from Ma Chivers. My magic alone may not be enough to thwart her, but if you add yours to it, then it should do the job. It will only last for a few weeks at the most, but that should be long enough to take us through to the Elite Competition."

"That sounds like a plan. When can you let me have the potion?"

"Drop by tomorrow afternoon, and it'll be ready for you to add your magic."

As I walked to the office, I thought about what Grandma had said. When I'd first discovered I was a witch, I'd been keen to work my way through the levels until I reached the pinnacle of level six. That no longer seemed important. I was now confident in my own abilities, and no longer needed a number to bolster my ego. Level four, six or even seven—what did it matter?

I'd spent far too much time worrying about my past. I'd

now resigned myself to never knowing for sure what connected me to either Magna Mondale or Juliet Braxmore. Was I a reincarnation of one or both of them? I had no idea, and would probably never know, but that was okay. At long last, I was comfortable in my own skin.

I'm me. I'm Jill Maxwell.

Chapter 19

"Did you see her?" Mrs V said, as soon as I walked into the office.

"See who?"

"The spy."

Oh boy, here we go again. "Which spy would that be, Mrs V?"

"She was hanging around on the street, near the entrance to the building. You must have spotted her; she's dressed as a parking warden."

"I did see the parking warden."

"What did I tell you? Those crocheters will stop at nothing."

"It's the same parking warden who's worked in this part of town for the last six months. She's there most mornings."

"Are you sure?"

"I'm positive. She gave me a ticket three months ago when I'd stopped to drop off some files at the office."

"Hmm." Mrs V didn't sound convinced.

If I was to tell you that Winky was no longer wearing the glasses and false moustache, you would probably think that common sense had prevailed.

But you'd be wrong.

"Why are you wearing that wig, Winky?"

"Drat! I didn't think you'd see through this disguise."

"Do you really think this is still necessary? Bruiser thinks you've gone away."

"Better safe than sorry. Maybe if I combined the glasses, false moustache *and* wig? What do you think?"

Before I could respond, my phone rang.

"Jill, it's Chris Longacre."

"Hi. Is everything okay?"

"Yes, thanks. I wanted to let you know that we've spoken to Mark and Susan, and they're both well. Physically, at least."

"How do you mean?"

"They're full of apologies for upsetting us like this, but neither of them can explain why they did what they did."

"Presumably they got carried away. You know what it's like when you're that age."

"Maybe, but that isn't the only odd thing. When they told us about some of the things they've been up to in London, a few of them didn't make any sense."

"Oh?"

"For example, they said they'd been walking on the South Bank, and that work on the London Eye was almost completed, but the Eye opened almost twenty years ago now."

Oh bum! When I'd implanted my memories of a day trip to London, it hadn't occurred to me that they might be a bit out of date.

"Perhaps it was closed for maintenance?"

"Maybe, but that's not the only odd thing. They insist they went to see Return to Music, but that show hasn't been on in the West End for almost eighteen years."

It was all coming back to me now. My adoptive parents had taken Kathy and me to London for the day, and in the evening, we'd been to the theatre, to see Return to Music.

"Maybe they got the name of the show mixed up. Mark and Susan are both okay, though, aren't they? That's the main thing."

"You're right, of course, but they've also managed to lose their train tickets for the journey home. I had to buy new ones for them. Anyway, none of this is your problem. We're just grateful you were able to track them down. You'll send me your invoice, I assume?"

"It'll be in the post tonight."

***

Charlie Cross had persuaded Rosemary Thorne, the police officer in charge of Myrtle's case, to spare me a few minutes. We met in The Boomerang, which was considerably busier than on my previous visit.

I arrived first, and after ordering my usual lime and soda, I found a quiet spot by a window, which looked out over the rear garden.

"Are you Jill Maxwell?"

The woman was younger than I'd expected—probably around my age. Smartly dressed, she had a no-nonsense air about her.

"That's me." I stood up and offered my hand, which she shook somewhat half-heartedly.

"This will have to be quick. I'm very busy."

"Of course. Can I get you a drink?"

"Not for me, thanks. I should tell you that I'm not in the habit of talking to private investigators. That's what you are, isn't it?"

"That's right."

"I'm doing this as a favour to Mr Cross."

"I appreciate you sparing the time. I've been hired by Myrtle Turtle."

"So I gathered. If you haven't done so already, you'll

soon realise this is an open and shut case."

"Maybe, but I'd still like to ask you a few questions if I may?"

"Fire away, but I can't guarantee that I'll be able to answer all of them. And like I said, I only have a few minutes to spare."

"Fair enough. I understand that you haven't yet found the murder weapon?"

"That's correct."

"Doesn't that worry you?"

"Finding it would certainly tie things up nicely, but I'm confident the evidence against Ms Turtle is strong enough without it."

"Isn't most of it circumstantial?"

"In my judgement, there's more than enough circumstantial evidence for a jury to convict her. There's no dispute that the deceased entered the river close to the waterwheel that is on Ms Turtle's property. His footprints were found in her back garden. The only access to that garden is through the house. And of course, the two of them were seen arguing earlier in the day."

"You'll pardon me for saying so, but that still sounds very flimsy. Even if we accept he was killed in Myrtle's back garden, who's to say someone else couldn't have done it?"

"Like who? No one else has access to her house except those two friends of hers, and they were both out of the village at the time the murder took place."

"What about Rob Evans' phone? Are there any records of calls he made or received just prior to his murder?"

"The phone has never been recovered from the river."

"But surely, if you —"

"I'm sorry. I really do have to get back to work now. Honestly, I think you're wasting your time on this one." And with that, she was gone.

I was about to leave too when I was joined by Hodd and Jobbs. I hadn't noticed them before then, but I suspected they'd been sitting somewhere close by.

"That was short and sweet," Hodd said.

"She's a woman of few words."

"We could have told you that you'd be wasting your time with that one. She's already made her mind up that Turtle's guilty."

"She may have difficulty getting a conviction without the murder weapon."

"You mean the poker," Jobbs said, in a hushed voice.

"Poker? I didn't think they knew what the murder weapon was?"

"*They* don't."

"How can you be sure it was a poker?"

"We're not one-hundred percent sure, but when we took a look around the house, we—"

"Hold on. I thought Myrtle's house was still off-limits. How did you get inside it if the police haven't released it?"

"We have our methods." Hodd gave me a knowing wink. "We wanted to see if we could find anything that might help Turtle."

"And did you?"

"Not really, except we noticed one of her brass pokers was missing."

"*One* of them?"

"Turtle collects them. It's sort of a hobby with her."

"I don't suppose you mentioned this to the police?"

"Of course not. It wouldn't help Turtle if they knew the murder weapon was one of her pokers, would it?"

"I suppose not."

"What else did Thorney have to say?" Hodd said.

"Nothing I didn't already know. I asked if they'd checked Rob Evans' phone records, but she said the phone hadn't been recovered. It's probably been washed away downstream by now. To be honest, she didn't seem to think it was important."

"Do you?"

"I don't know. It might have been."

"We can get the records off it if it would help?" Jobbs said.

"How?"

"Best you don't know."

"Okay. It can't do any harm."

"Consider it done."

***

"I think they managed to get into your office, Jill," Mrs V said.

"Who did?"

"One of the crochet spies."

Sigh.

"What makes you think that?"

"I went through there to feed the stupid cat, and I found these." She held up the wig, the pair of plastic glasses and the false moustache. "They must have been here in disguise."

"Those don't belong to the crocheters, they belong to—

err—" I suddenly realised what I was about to say.

"Who?"

"Err, me—they're mine."

"Yours? I know you have to work undercover sometimes, but these aren't going to fool anyone."

"No, they're—err—was that my phone ringing?"

"I didn't hear anything."

"I think it was." I grabbed the wig, glasses and moustache, and then bolted for my office.

"She's a thief!" Winky yelled.

"Sorry?"

"The old bag lady. She stole my disguise."

"It's all here. Keep these somewhere out of sight, will you? And whatever you do, don't let Mrs V see you wearing this lot. Even I couldn't explain that away."

***

It was mid-afternoon, and I was at a bit of a loose end. Until Hodd and Jobbs got back to me with the phone records for Rob Evans, there wasn't much else I could do on Myrtle's case. I was on the point of giving myself the rest of the day off when my phone rang.

The voice was so quiet, I couldn't make out who it was or what they were saying.

"You'll have to speak up. I can't hear you."

"It's Sarah, from Coffee Games. Can you hear me now?"

"Only just."

"I daren't speak any louder or he might hear."

"Who might?"

"You told me to be on the lookout for anyone trying to get us to sell blood. Well, there's a vampire in here now.

He reckons he runs the blood distribution network, and he's just asked if we'd consider selling blood in the shop."

"What did you tell him?"

"That I'd have to go and get the boss. That's where he thinks I am now."

"Can you keep him talking for a few more minutes until I get down there?"

"I'll try."

"What does he look like?"

"He's wearing a purple tie."

"Okay, I'm on my way."

"Hurry, Jill, I'm not sure I'll be able to keep him talking for long. Not once he knows the boss isn't actually here today."

"I'm coming now."

As soon as I was out of the building, I cast the 'faster' spell, and then sped down the high street to Coffee Games. I arrived just in time to see a man, with a purple tie, step out of the door.

I considered confronting him there and then, but I had no evidence of any wrongdoing. It would be his word against Sarah's. Instead, I decided to follow him. If I could find out where he was based, I could let Daze know. She could then handle it however she thought best.

I half-expected him to get into a car, which would have caused me a few problems, but instead, he walked to one of the new apartment blocks close to the town hall. I followed him inside, made a note of his apartment number, and then contacted Daze.

"Thanks, Jill, that's great. We'll pay him a visit shortly. We're bound to find some evidence in his flat."

I phoned Mrs V.

"I'm not going to bother coming back to the office. I'll see you in the morning."

"Is everything okay? I was a little worried when you rushed out without a word."

"Everything's fine. I just needed a coffee."

"I worry about that caffeine habit of yours."

"It's okay. I had decaf. I'll see you tomorrow."

It was nice to finish early, and as it was such a beautiful day, I planned to relax in the garden with a good book.

"Jill!"

Oh no! I'd just pulled onto the drive when Mr Ivers came scurrying across.

"Hello, Monty."

"I wanted to check that you haven't forgotten."

"Err, no. Of course not." What was he talking about?

"Good. Make sure you're early because I'm expecting a large crowd."

The penny dropped. "Oh yeah, the opening of your new shop. It's this week, isn't it?"

"Tomorrow morning."

"That soon?"

"Yes. At nine o'clock. Charlie Barley has confirmed, so it's all systems go."

"Fantastic." Yawnsville.

"The local TV and radio will be there."

"Really? Do you think they'll want to interview people in the crowd?"

"They've said they want to speak to me, and to Charlie, but I suppose it's always possible. Why?"

"No reason, but if they do, you'll want to be sure it's someone articulate who can speak positively about the prospects for your business, won't you?"

"I suppose so."

"I'd be happy to volunteer. You can tell them they're welcome to speak to me if they wish."

"That's very kind of you. Thank you very much."

"My pleasure."

Who said I didn't understand marketing? Once in front of the microphone and camera, I'd quickly drop a few platitudes about the internet café, and then namecheck my business. Was I brilliant or what?

What have I told you? I refer you once again to the entry in the dictionary for the word: Rhetorical.

Chapter 20

The next morning, Jack, Alicia and I were all in the kitchen.

"What would you like for breakfast, Alicia?" I took the packet of sausages from the fridge. "I'm going to have a sausage cob. Or I suppose you could always have some of Jack's muesli." I laughed.

"I'd love some muesli, thanks."

I thought at first that she was joking, but then I realised she was being serious.

Another freak!

"There you go." Jack passed Alicia a bowl of sawdust.

"I still can't believe you're going to Ivers' shindig this morning," he said.

"I hadn't intended to until I discovered the local TV and radio were going to be there."

"They'll be there for Charlie what's-his-name and his onions."

"Barley, and it's carrots, not onions."

"They still won't have any interest in you."

"Don't be so sure about that. I intend to get in a plug for my business if it kills me."

After Jack had gone upstairs, Alicia said, "Don't take this the wrong way, Jill, but I'll be glad to get out of here."

"Grandma said the potion should be ready today, so with a bit of luck, you'll be able to leave tonight."

***

As I was going straight to the grand opening of Have Ivers Got Internet For You, I left the house much later than Jack. I was about to get into the car when I had a phone call from Daze.

"I hope I haven't caught you still in bed." I could hear the grin in her voice.

Why did people keep saying that? "I'll have you know that I've been up for ages. How did you get on yesterday?"

"That's why I called, actually. It was a complete bust."

"Why, what went wrong?"

"We went to his apartment, but I knew as soon as he welcomed us inside that we were on a loser. The place was definitely clean. We turned it upside down, but there wasn't a scrap of evidence to link him to the blood distribution network. He did have a few bottles of blood in his fridge, but it was only enough for his own consumption. We took a bottle away and tested it, just to be sure, but it wasn't contaminated."

"I guess that leaves you back at square one?"

"Worse than that. Now he knows we're onto him, he's unlikely to do anything incriminating until he believes things have died down."

"I know it's not the result you were hoping for, but at least it might stop the supply of contaminated blood."

"I'd settle for that, but somehow I doubt it. My guess is he'll still be able to orchestrate the operation."

"What's your plan, then?"

"I wish I had one. Short of a confession, there's not much else we can do."

"What's this guy's name?"

"Rory Storey."

"I've got an idea that might just see Mr Storey brought to justice."

I outlined my plan, and Daze gave it her blessing, so as soon as I'd finished on the call, I phoned my old friend Bob Bobb who agreed to see me later.

***

I had to hand it to Mr Ivers, he'd spared no expense on the grand opening of his new business. Not only had he engaged the 'celebrity' Charlie (where's my carrot) Barley, he'd also booked a brass band who had set up on the pavement outside the shop. While they played some awful tune or other, a number of young men and women, dressed in yellow and orange blazers, moved among the crowd, handing out goodie-bags.

I'd badly misjudged how big a crowd the event would attract. Charlie Barley was obviously more popular than I'd thought. The free champagne must also have been an attraction. Speaking of which, I decided to claim my free glass of bubbly.

"I'll have a glass, please."

"Do you have your carrot?"

"Sorry?"

"Everyone who's brought a carrot gets a free glass of champers."

"I left my carrot in the car."

"Sorry."

"Couldn't you make an exception? You seem to have plenty of bottles."

"That wouldn't be fair to those who *did* remember their carrot, would it?"

"Fine. I didn't want one anyway."

I spotted Mr Ivers; he was standing near to the shop

entrance, but I wasn't able to catch his eye because of the large number of people in front of me. There was zero chance of my being on TV and radio unless I could somehow make it to the front.

My attempts to barge my way through proved fruitless, so a different approach was called for. Making myself invisible wouldn't have done any good because I'd still have the problem of having to force my way through to the front. I considered simply transporting myself to the door, but that was fraught with problems, so instead, I opted to shrink myself to the size of a small bug. I would have to be very careful as I weaved my way through the feet of the crowd. One wrong move and I'd be squashed. I'd also have to keep my eyes peeled for any hungry spiders.

Phew! I'd made it unscathed to the front, but I couldn't reverse the spell just yet because there were way too many witnesses. Fortunately, the door behind Mr Ivers was ajar, so I made my way inside. Once I was at the back of the shop, and out of sight, I reverted to full size.

"Morning, Monty."

Mr Ivers spun around and did a double take.

"Jill? Where did you come from?"

"You did say that I should arrive early. I was here before everyone else, and as the door was ajar, I took a quick look inside. I hope you don't mind?"

"Err—no, of course not. I wasn't sure you'd even bother coming."

"What? I wouldn't have missed this for the world."

"Charlie Barley should be here any minute now."

"What about the TV and radio people?"

"I'm expecting them soon."

"Excellent. You won't forget what we spoke about, will you? I'll be glad to say a few words about your new venture."

"Of course. I do appreciate you doing this, Jill."

"Think nothing of it. That's what neighbours are for."

Ten minutes later, Carrot Man arrived, to much applause. He was a rather unremarkable man who looked more like a turnip than a carrot. The TV crew had also arrived, and I was close enough to them to hear the conversation between the director, Mr Ivers and Charlie Barley. The director had come up with the idea of staging a mini game of Where's My Carrot, inside the shop. Mr Ivers seemed keen, and Charlie confirmed that he never went anywhere without his carrot or file of questions.

"We'll do an interview with the winner," the director said. "Monty, if you could pick out three contestants, we can get the ball rolling."

"Will do!" Mr Ivers turned to the crowd.

"Monty!" I practically pushed the TV director out of the way. "Monty! I'll do it."

"Are you sure, Jill? I didn't think you'd seen the programme?"

"Whatever gave you that idea? I love Where's My Carrot. It's the best thing on TV."

"Well, if you're sure?"

"Absolutely."

He picked two other contestants from the crowd: an elderly woman and a schoolboy. The three of us went into the shop, accompanied by the film crew. The standard of my competition was laughable. I'd have this won in no time, and then it would be my big interview and a chance to plug my business.

Grandma eat your heart out—meet Jill Maxwell, marketing guru.

"Right," Charlie Barley said, once the two other competitors and I were lined up inside the shop. "I assume you're all familiar with the game format?"

The other two nodded. I was just about to say I'd never seen the show when I remembered I'd told Mr Ivers that it was my favourite programme, so I kept quiet.

Charlie continued, "In the show, there would usually be several rounds, but today there will only be one. In fact, there'll be just a single question—solve it and it will lead you to the carrot. Are you ready?"

The other competitors were straining at the bit, but I was more concerned about making sure the camera got my good side. It's not like I had anything to worry about. How difficult could it be to outthink a slip of a kid and a sweet old dear?

"Here's your clue." Charlie handed us each a piece of paper.

Where a small rodent might hide.

What on earth did a rodent have to do with a carrot? Rabbits liked carrots, but I was fairly sure they weren't rodents. This was more difficult than I'd expected, but I was still feeling confident.

"Found it!" The young boy held the carrot aloft.

"Well done, young man," Charlie said. "You're the winner."

"Where was the carrot?" I asked Mr Ivers.

"Under one of the mouse mats."

"What does a mouse have to do with a carrot?"

"The clue was: *where a small rodent might hide.*"

"That's stupid." I was disappointed at not having won, but the stupid carrot game wasn't the reason I was there. "When will they want me to do my interview?"

"I don't think they will. They're only going to talk to the winner."

"But he's just a kid."

"Sorry, Jill."

So much for my chance to plug my business on TV. The crowd had made their way into the shop, so I sneaked away. It had been an unmitigated disaster, but at least no one except Mr Ivers had seen my miserable performance.

"Jill!" Grandma called to me, as I walked past Ever. "I have that potion for you." She led the way to her office.

"Is that it?" I stared at the dark brown liquid in the small jam jar. "It looks horrible."

"It smells even worse."

"I guess it has to look and smell bad in order to work."

"Actually, it doesn't. It starts out as an odourless clear liquid. I add the colouring and smell for effect." She unscrewed the lid, and the smell hit me.

"That's awful."

"I need you to cast this spell to give the potion enough strength." She pointed to the spell book that was open on her desk.

I did as she asked, so that she'd hurry up and replace the lid.

"Thanks for this, Grandma." I put the jar in my bag. "I'd better get going."

"And thank you, Jill, for the entertainment."

"Sorry?"

"I haven't laughed so much in a long time."

"I have no idea what you're talking about."

"Don't be shy, little mouse."

"You saw that?"

"I did, and I have to say it was hilarious, watching that young kid hand your backside to you."

"I didn't notice you down at the shop."

"I wasn't there. I watched it live on TV."

"It went out live?"

"It most certainly did."

Oh bum!

***

"I'm sorry I didn't warn you I'd be in late, Mrs V."

"That's alright, dear. I knew where you were."

"You did? How?"

"Kathy rang to ask if I'd seen you on TV."

"She saw it?"

"Yes, she said it was one of the funniest things she's seen for ages."

"It wasn't all that funny."

"I'll be able to judge for myself when I get home tonight. I've asked Armi to record it for me."

"Great."

Winky was fast asleep on the sofa, or so I thought.

"Where's my food?" he said.

"Give me a chance. I've only just walked through the door. I suppose you'll be wanting salmon?"

"Actually, I quite fancy some carrots." He dissolved into

laughter and rolled off the sofa.

"How did you — never mind — I don't want to know."

"Beaten by a schoolkid. Clients will be queuing around the block to hire you now."

"It was the pressure. I couldn't think straight."

Five minutes later, Winky was still chuckling to himself when my phone rang.

"Jill, it's Jobbs. Do you know what I've just been looking at?"

"Let me guess. You've been watching early morning TV?" Was there anyone who hadn't seen me making a fool of myself?

"What? No. I've been looking through Rob Evans' phone records."

"Anything interesting?"

"Potentially, yes. There's a message from Sydney's phone an hour after Evans left the pub."

"When I spoke to Sydney, she maintained that she hadn't been able to get in touch with him that day because she'd lost her phone. Do you know what the message said?"

"No. Just that there was a message."

"I think I need to have another word with that young lady."

"Would you like Hodd and me to accompany you? We can be very persuasive in getting people to talk."

"Thanks for the offer, but that won't be necessary."

I'd thought at the time that something didn't ring true about Sydney's claim to have lost her phone. It was beginning to look like my gut feeling was right. What had she been trying to hide? What had been in that message to Rob Evans?

Chapter 21

I was going to see Bob Bobb, the bigxie I'd recently helped when he was having problems with a rogue trader who'd been poaching his customers. I was hoping that Bob would be able to help with our mission to put the blood distribution network out of business.

First, though, a coffee and muffin were the order of the day. Pearl and Mindy were both behind the counter in Cuppy C.

"My usual, please."

"Sorry, Jill? What did you say?"

It was hardly surprising that Pearl couldn't hear me because of all the banging coming from upstairs.

"What's going on up there?" I shouted.

She shook her head to indicate she still couldn't hear, but then gestured for me to follow her into the back where it was a little quieter.

"What's going on?"

"We've got the builders in."

"Already? You two don't let the grass grow, do you?"

"You said yourself that the creche was a good idea, so there was no point in hanging around."

"I suppose not. I'm just surprised you found someone who was able to start so quickly."

"We hit lucky." She pointed through the window to a white van parked in the alleyway.

"Cutt Corners?"

"Yeah, they'd had a cancellation, so they were able to start work straight away."

"But that name? Didn't that ring any alarm bells?"

"That's their surnames, silly." She laughed. "Roger Cutt

and Colin Corners. They're really nice guys."

"And you checked their references I assume?"

"No one trusts references anymore; they're so easily faked. Amber and I interviewed them, and we both agreed they seemed like genuine guys."

The hammering stopped, and two men, both vampires, came down the stairs. Pearl made the introductions.

"Jill, this is Roger Cutt, and this is Colin Corners. Jill is our cousin."

"Nice to meet you both," I said.

"You too." Roger brushed the dust off his overalls. "This is one of the best jobs we've ever had. Your cousins' cakes are fantastic."

"I was just remarking to Pearl that your company name is a bit unfortunate for a pair of builders."

"Oh? Why's that?" Colin said.

They both looked puzzled.

"You know: cut corners. No one wants their builder to do that."

"It had never occurred to me," Roger said.

"Me neither." Colin shook his head. "We could always make it Corners Cutt. Do you think that would be better?"

Oh boy!

After the two guys had gone through to the shop, Pearl turned on me. "There was no need to have a go at them, Jill."

"I wasn't. I was only pointing out that their choice of company name was unfortunate. I can't believe they hadn't worked that out for themselves before now. Anyway, how long is the work going to take?"

"A couple of weeks, they reckon. We can't wait to open the creche."

"Who's going to look after the kids?"

"The parents will stay up there with their children, but we're planning to hire someone to help out too. You wouldn't be interested in the job, would you?"

"Me?"

"It's okay, I'm only joking. I remember how traumatised you were after having to look after the babies for a day."

It was true. When Aunt Lucy and the twins had gone down with sup flu, I'd been 'volunteered' to babysit Lil and Lily. Without a shadow of a doubt, that day had been harder work than any case I'd ever worked on.

***

"I didn't expect to see you again so soon, Jill." Bob Bobb was sporting an argyle pattern jumper and plus-fours.

"I appreciate you seeing me at such short notice. I must say you're looking particularly dapper today, Bob."

"Thanks. I have a round of golf planned for later. Do you play?"

"Golf? Me? Not really my thing."

"What's your sport?"

"Jack occasionally drags me to the ten-pin bowling alley, but that's about it."

"You mentioned something about contaminated blood when we spoke on the phone?"

"That's right. The rogue retrievers were recently successful in closing down a blood distribution network in Washbridge, but it's resurfaced, and this time, they have precious little quality control. A number of vampires have already died after drinking the bad blood."

"What exactly do you need from me?"

"We're fairly certain we've identified the new Mr Big who's now in charge of the operation, but there isn't any evidence for the rogue retrievers to act against him. That's where you come in."

"Okay?"

"I have his details, and I was hoping that you could check your records to see if by any chance you provide your services to him."

"Sure. No problem."

I gave him the vampire's name and address, and waited while he checked his computer.

"Storey, Rory. Yes, we do."

"That's fantastic. Would you be willing to help put him away?"

"I wouldn't normally entertain the idea of acting against one of our clients, but from what you've just told me, this man's actions could well be responsible for killing off even more of our customers. I'm in."

"Great. What about the bigxies assigned to him? Will they co-operate?"

"They will after I've explained the situation. How do you want to play this, Jill?"

I told Bob what I had in mind, and he said he'd put the wheels in motion.

***

I was about to magic myself back to Washbridge when I got a call from Aunt Lucy.

"Pearl said you were over here. Can I ask a favour?"

"Sure. What is it?"

"Is there any chance you could take Barry for a walk?

Dot was supposed to be coming to collect him, but she called a few minutes ago to say her verruca is playing up, so she can't make it today. I'd take him myself, but I've just got Lily settled."

"No problem. I'll be there in a couple of minutes."

How could I say no? After all, Barry was supposed to be my dog, and I didn't walk him half as often as I should have done.

"Can we go for a walk, Jill?" Barry had me pinned to the door.

"Yes, but only if you get down."

"Sorry, but I love going for walks."

"I kind of gathered that."

"Rhymes says he doesn't like walks. I think that's daft."

"He is a lot slower than you."

"That's what I thought, but he always says that I'm a bit on the slow side."

"Hmm, come on. Let's go to the park."

"I love the park!"

***

It was a warm day, and by the time we got there, I was ready for a sit down, but the benches were all occupied. As soon as I let Barry off his lead he ran off, and was soon out of sight. I didn't worry about that as much as I used to because I knew he would eventually come charging back to me.

As I got a little further into the park, I noticed that dozens of deckchairs had been set up on some of the large expanses of grass. What a brilliant idea, and just what I needed while Barry ran off his excess energy. As all the benches were full, I was rather surprised that no one seemed to have taken advantage of the deckchairs.

A relaxing hour spent sunbathing in a deckchair was just what the doctor ordered.

Hold on a minute! What the — ?

I'd only just spotted the sign, propped against a tree, which read:

Deckchair hire - £10 per day.

Were they having a laugh?

"It's a joke, isn't it?" The old man standing close to me shook his head. "Who's going to pay ten pounds to sit in a deckchair?"

"Not me, that's for sure. Anyway, how are they going to know if you've paid or not?" I grinned. "I've a good mind to sit in one."

"I wouldn't do that if I were you. They've employed a warden to collect the charges, and she's a real ogre. I just saw her down the other end of the park."

"Right. Thanks for the tip-off."

There was no way I was going to pay for a deckchair, but I really did need to rest my feet for a while. I checked the benches again; they were all still occupied, but on one of them was a woman seated all by herself. That should have left room for at least another two people if she hadn't decided to put her shopping bags on there too.

"Excuse me. Is anyone sitting here?"

"I am."

"I can see that. I meant is *anyone else* sitting here?"

The smartass then proceeded to look left and right before saying, "I don't see anyone."

"In that case, perhaps you wouldn't mind moving your bags, so I can sit down?"

She grumbled under her breath, but she did at least put one of the bags on the floor, so I could squeeze on beside her.

In an attempt to forge a truce, I tried to make small talk.

"Beautiful day isn't it?"

Grunt.

"I'm here with my dog, Barry."

"I hate dogs."

"Do you come to the park often?"

"No because whenever I do, some stranger thinks I want to talk to them."

Now, in my defence, I was hot, tired and worried about Myrtle's case. That is still no excuse for doing what I did, but it has to be said, she made a much better toad than she had a human.

Obviously, I reversed the spell after a couple of minutes, and cast the 'forget' spell so she wouldn't remember her ordeal.

What? Come on — I was totally provoked.

I was starting to get a little worried about Barry when he came charging up to me, and planted his paws in my lap.

"Did you enjoy that, boy?"

"I did. I love the park, but I'm hungry now."

"In that case, we'd better get you back home." I clipped on his lead, bid farewell to my new friend (who didn't even manage a croak in response), and then headed for the gates.

"Excuse me." A large woman stepped out in front of us;

she was wearing a blue uniform: Her blazer was several sizes too large; her trousers were at least three inches too short. "You haven't paid yet."

"Paid for what?"

"The deckchair hire."

"I didn't sit in a deckchair. I've been sitting on that bench over there."

"I didn't mean you."

"Sorry? If you didn't mean *me*, then why have you stopped *me*?"

"Because your dog has been sitting in a deckchair for the last fifteen minutes."

"Don't be ridiculous. Barry wouldn't even be able to get into a deckchair."

"Really?" She held out her phone for me to see, and sure enough, there was a photo of Barry, relaxing in a deckchair. "That'll be ten pounds, please."

"You can't charge me for a dog."

"I think you'll find I can. It's right there in the small print. The charge is the same regardless of who occupies the chair. Ten pounds, please."

I seriously considered turning her into a toad too, but there were too many witnesses around. Instead, I was forced to hand over the cash.

"I like the park," Barry said, as we made our way home. "Those new chairs are really nice."

***

After dropping Barry back at Aunt Lucy's house, I magicked myself back to the office.

I toyed with the idea of sorting out my invoices, but

couldn't be bothered, so instead, I tidied my desk drawers. I never failed to be amazed at some of the stuff I found in there. For the life of me, I couldn't remember buying that fitness DVD.

Winky, who until now had been lazing on the sofa, suddenly jumped to his feet. The fur on his back was standing on end, and there was an unmistakeable look of terror on his face. When I glanced over at the window, I understood why.

"Bruiser, I can explain." Winky hadn't donned his disguise that day—not that it would have done much good. "It wasn't my fault. Please don't hurt me."

"Don't worry about it, mate." Bruiser jumped down from the window sill. "No hard feelings."

"Are you sure? I thought you'd be mad about the—err—"

"Tattoo? It's still a bit inflamed, but I've had worse."

"That's very understanding of you, Bruiser."

"We felines have to be understanding of one another, don't we, Winky?"

"Absolutely. I couldn't agree more."

"I'm pleased you feel that way." He turned around and called out, "Crystal, come on in."

Moments later, she appeared in the window, and then jumped down to join Bruiser.

"Crystal?" Winky stared at her. "What are you doing here?"

"She's with me now," Bruiser said. "I know you must be disappointed, but like you said, we all have to be understanding of one another, don't we?"

"I—err—but why, Crystal?"

"Sorry, Winky." She didn't sound it. "What can I say?

Bruiser is a great guy, and the flat where he lives puts this place to shame. It has the most gorgeous sofa."

"But Crystal," Winky pleaded.

"Time to man up and accept you've lost out, Winky." Bruiser put his paw around Crystal.

After they'd left, Winky looked so desolate that I felt I had to try and cheer him up.

"She was never right for you, Winky. There are plenty more fish—"

"This is all your fault! If you'd spent some money on this place instead of buying fitness DVDs, she never would have left me."

Chapter 22

When I got up the next morning, I expected to find Alicia in the kitchen, but she was nowhere to be seen. On the assumption she must still be asleep, I went through to the lounge.

Oh no!

She was lying on the floor with her eyes open, staring at the ceiling. The empty jam jar, which had contained the potion, was on the coffee table. This was terrible. Grandma must have got the potion wrong, and now Alicia was dead.

I crouched down next to her. What had I done? This was all my fault.

"Boo!" She sat up, sending me tumbling backwards.

"Are you insane? I could have had a heart attack."

"Sorry, Jill." She put her hand on my arm. "Being stuck in this house for so long has sent me stir-crazy. I had to do something to entertain myself."

"I see that you managed to drink all of the potion last night, then?" I hadn't been able to bring myself to watch her drink the foul concoction.

"Only just, but it did make me retch a few times."

"I guess you'll be leaving us now?"

"Yeah, and I can't thank you enough for what you've done. If there's ever anything I can do for you, don't hesitate to ask."

"Do you know where you'll go?"

"I'm not sure, but I need to get far away from Washbridge."

"What about your house next door to my Aunt Lucy? And what about Glen?"

"Glen and I split up a while ago. It was probably my fault. With all this business with Ma Chivers, I haven't been myself. We'd only rented the house, anyway, so that won't be a problem. I have to get away from here; I need a new start somewhere else."

***

Bob Bobb had been as good as his word. He'd arranged for me to meet with Simon Simons, one of the bigxies who provided Rory Storey with a mirror image service.

We met in Coffee and Socks, a small coffee shop close to the town hall. It was my first visit to that particular establishment, and I have to confess that the name of the shop had me puzzled.

"A caramel latte, please."

"Anything to eat with that?"

I was tempted by the muffins, but I hadn't long since had breakfast. "No, thanks. Do I get socks with this?"

"I'm afraid not. Just coffee."

"I take it you get asked that a lot?"

"You wouldn't believe how often. The owner changed the name of the shop recently, but I have no idea why he chose it. I really wish he'd come up with a better name, or at least explained why he'd chosen to call it socks."

"Didn't you ask him?"

"Yeah. He said it was none of my business. Between you and me, he's a bit of an idiot."

Just then, someone tapped me on the shoulder.

"Jill?"

"Simon?"

"Yes. Pleased to meet you."

Unlike their close relatives, the pixies, the bigxies were tall enough that they could pass amongst humans unnoticed.

"Would you like a drink, Simon?"

"Hot chocolate, please."

"Okay. Why don't you find a table, and I'll bring the drinks over?"

"I'm a little nervous about all this." Simon took a sip of his drink, leaving a chocolate moustache on his upper lip.

"There's really nothing to worry about. I'll be right there with you."

"But won't he see you?"

"No. I'll make myself invisible just before we go into the apartment together. Did Bob Bobb tell you the plan?"

"Yeah. I'm just worried I might mess up."

"You'll be fine. Does Rory shave every morning?"

"Yeah, regular as clockwork."

"What about the blood? The plan will only work if he's recently had a drink."

"That won't be a problem. He always drinks a bottleful of that horrible stuff just before he shaves. I know that because he sometimes brings the bottle into the bathroom with him, and he occasionally has drops of blood on his lips. It's disgusting."

"That's great. Do you have any questions?"

"Just one. I'm not sure what the boils are supposed to look like."

"I have a photo of one of the victims, but I should warn you that it isn't pretty." I took out my phone, and showed him the photo that Daze had send to me.

"Oh dear. That's much worse than I imagined."

"You see now why we have to put this guy out of business."

He nodded. "I won't let you down."

Ten minutes later, we were at Rory Storey's apartment. After I'd made myself invisible, Simon rang the doorbell.

"You're late!" Rory Storey snapped at Simon.

"Sorry, it's only a couple of minutes. The traffic was—"

"I'm not interested in your excuses. I have places to go and people to meet. If this happens again, I shall ask the agency for a replacement."

After Rory Storey had disappeared into his bedroom, Simon and I headed for the bathroom, which was large and very luxurious—no doubt financed by his evil trade in contaminated blood.

When Rory came through to the bathroom, he had a few drops of blood on his lower lip—just as Simon had predicted he would. Remarkably, in the blink of an eye, Simon's mirror image of Rory had those same drops of blood on his lip. I was still astonished at how easily the bigxies could transform into their client's mirror image.

Rory was oblivious to the fact that I was standing in the corner of the bathroom. As I'd instructed, Simon waited until Rory began to shave, then, gradually, the green boils began to appear on Simon's mirror image of Rory. At first there were just two on his forehead. Then several more appeared on his cheeks.

"What's happening?" Rory took several steps back. "No! No!"

That was my cue to reverse the 'invisible' spell. "Oh dear. You don't look at all well."

"Who are you?"

"I'm your only hope."

"I don't understand." He stared in horror at the mirror where his reflection was now covered in green boils.

"It looks as though someone must have swapped your bottles of blood. I wonder who could have done that."

"You!" He lashed out at me, but I easily avoided his punch. "You did this to me!"

"And I'm the only one who can save you."

"What do you mean? There is no cure for this."

"Actually, there is. Our chemists have analysed the blood of those vampires who died after drinking your contaminated product, and they've managed to develop an antidote."

"Give it to me! Quick!"

"I'm not sure I should."

"Please, I'll do anything."

"Anything? Are you sure?"

"Yes, just give me the antidote before it's too late."

"Okay. Wait there. I'll go and get it."

I hurried back downstairs, and opened the door to the apartment building. As arranged, Daze was waiting outside.

"How did it go?" she said.

"Like a dream. Did you bring the 'antidote'?"

"You mean this?" She grinned and held out a small bottle containing what I knew to be water.

"Okay. Let's go and see what this guy has to say for himself."

"Who's this?" Rory glared at Daze.

"This is my friend, Daze. And, in case you haven't already worked it out, she's a rogue retriever. You're going to tell her all about the blood distribution network, and then she'll give you the antidote."

"No, give me that first!" He made a grab for it, but Daze moved out of his reach.

"No antidote for you until we have a full confession."

"Okay, okay." Rory Storey confessed to everything, and gave Daze the names of all of his associates. And he did so in lightning fast time. "Now give me the antidote before it's too late."

Daze handed him the bottle and he gulped it down.

"That tasted like water. Are you sure it will work?"

"See for yourself." I pointed to the mirror where Simon's mirror image of Rory was now boil-free.

"Thank goodness." Rory sank to his knees with relief. "I thought I was a goner."

"Thanks for your help, Jill." Daze turned to Simon. "Thank you too." She took out her net, and threw it over Rory, who disappeared in a puff of smoke. "I'd better go and process that lowlife."

"Bye, Daze."

Simon had by now reverted to his own image.

"You did brilliantly, Simon."

"Thanks, Jill. My heart was racing so fast that I thought I was going to pass out."

"I'm sorry if this has put you and your colleagues out of a job."

"Don't give it a second thought. It was worth it to put that monster behind bars, and besides, Bob Bobb has already said he has another job lined up for us."

"Great. Thanks again."

***

It was time to pay another visit to Rob Evans' house in Middle Tweaking. I was hoping to catch his girlfriend, Sydney, to confront her about the text message that had been found on Rob's phone.

"You again?"

She was clearly pleased to see me.

"I just have a couple more questions for you."

"I'm busy."

"It'll only take a minute."

"I'm supposed to meet Mazza in Washbridge. The bus is in five minutes, and they only run every couple of hours."

"How about I give you a lift there? We can talk as I drive."

She considered it for a moment. "Okay, then, but you'll have to wait while I get changed."

"No problem." I was about to follow her into the house when she slammed the door in my face. Presumably, that was her way of telling me to wait outside.

"Hello there!" The man's voice startled me. "What brings you back to the village?"

"Hi." I couldn't place him at first, but then the smell of fish hit me. "It's Brendan, isn't it?"

"It is indeed. I must apologise for my behaviour the last time you were here. I'd been going through a bit of a rough patch."

Brendan Breeze was the village fishmonger. Myrtle and I had spoken to him about Madge Hick's murder. At the time, he'd been in something of a depression because Madge was an old flame of his. Brendan had berated himself for dumping Madge in favour of a younger model, Suzy, who had subsequently walked out on him.

"You look a lot better than the last time I saw you, Brendan."

"I am, and it's all down to Carmen; she's my new lady friend. We met online."

"Nice. Which dating web site did you use?"

"Plenty of Fishmongers."

"I take it she's in the same line of business?"

"Yes. Her parents were both fishmongers too."

"That's great."

"Are we going, then?" Sydney was back. "I don't want to be late."

"I'm coming. Nice to see you again, Brendan."

"Mazza reckons they've got a sale on makeup at Luvface," Sydney informed me, as we drove towards Washbridge.

"Nice."

"I suppose you need a lot of makeup at your age, don't you?"

Where was the ejector seat when you needed one?

"I wanted to ask you about the message you sent to Rob on the day he was murdered."

"I didn't send no message. I told you — my phone went missing that day."

"That's what you said, but I've seen Rob's phone records, and there was a message from you about an hour after he left The Boomerang."

"There can't have been. I didn't have my phone."

"Do you mind if I check it for myself?"

"Help yourself." She took it from her handbag. "You won't find anything."

I pulled into a layby, took the phone from her and scrolled through the messages. "What about this one?" I held it out for her to see.

"I didn't send that!"

"Well someone did."

It read: *Let's trash Turtle's place. Meet me there in five minutes.*

She snatched the phone back, and double-checked the message. "It wasn't me who sent that. I'd lost my phone that day. Just ask Mazza."

"Okay, I will. Let's go and talk to her."

After I'd parked the car, I followed Sydney to LuvFace, a small shop in the trendier part of town. As you might imagine, that was not an area I was particularly well acquainted with.

The young woman waiting outside LuvFace looked like she'd spent the last hour sampling every product that the shop had to offer.

"Hi, babes." She air-kissed Sydney, and then looked at me as though I was a creature from outer space.

"Tell her I lost my phone, Mazza."

"What, babes?"

"The day that Rob got done. I'd lost my phone, hadn't I? Do you remember? I told you when you came around to my place in the evening."

"Yeah, I remember now. Syd was really cut up about it. She couldn't check her Instagram or anything." Mazza looked me up and down again. "You probably don't even know what Instagram is, do you?"

"I do, actually."

"We're going now." Sydney grabbed Mazza's arm.

"They'll have sold out of all the good stuff soon."

"One last question. Where and when did you find your phone?"

"My aunt found it the next morning. It was in the house somewhere."

"In her house? Had you been to visit her?"

"No, I live there. My dad took off before I was born, and my mum died when I was a toddler. My aunt brought me up."

"So when you said you were at home the day that Rob was murdered, you were at your aunt's place?"

"That's what I said, isn't it? You can check with her if you like."

"Fred's really cool," Mazza said. "I wish my parents were like her."

"Fred? I thought you said it was your aunt?"

"She is my aunt, but I've always called her Fred." Sydney turned her back to me to indicate we were done.

I didn't mind that she'd rushed off because, at long last, I thought I might have caught a break on Myrtle's case.

Chapter 23

After I'd run some checks to confirm my hunch about Sydney's aunt, I went back to the car, and was about to drive to 'Fred's' when my phone rang. It was Ms Nightingale from CASS.

"Morning, Ms Nightingale. No more problems with the airship, I hope?"

"No. I'm pleased to report that everything has been plain sailing since you intervened. You're due to give a lesson here tomorrow, I believe?"

"Err? Yes, that's right." Oh bum! I'd forgotten all about that. I really would have to get more organised with my diary—as in buy one!

"I wondered if you might be able to spare me some time after you've finished teaching for the day?"

"Of course. Can you give me some idea of what it's about?"

"It's a rather delicate matter that I'd prefer not to discuss over the phone."

"I understand. Shall I pop by your office when I'm done in class?"

"Yes, please."

"Okay, I'll see you tomorrow."

I was intrigued. What could the headmistress want to talk to me about that she didn't feel she could discuss over the phone? I'd heard rumours that she was going to retire—could that be it?

"Hello again?" Freda Bowling looked surprised to see me. Thankfully, she didn't have the two curlers in her hair to distract me this time. "I wasn't expecting you, was I?"

"No. I'm sorry to turn up out of the blue, but I wondered if you might spare me a few minutes?"

"Of course. Come in. Can I get you a drink?"

"No, thanks. I was wondering, how long did you clean for Myrtle?"

"Just a few weeks."

"How was the work?"

"It was one of my easier jobs. Myrtle's house was pretty much spotless, even before I started work. Not like some of the places I go to. I could tell you stories that would make your toes curl."

"I'm sure, but when I was last at Myrtles', I noticed she had a lot of brass ornaments. They must have been a pain to keep clean?"

"She wouldn't let me clean her ornaments. She said she preferred to do those herself."

"You didn't get to clean her collection of pokers, then?"

Freda seemed to flinch—just a little, but she quickly recovered. "No, I never did. Are you sure you wouldn't like a drink?"

"Positive. Actually, just before I came here today, I gave your niece a lift to Washbridge."

"Oh?"

"Sydney is your niece, isn't she?"

"More like my daughter, really. I brought her up after her mother died."

"She said she calls you Fred?"

"That's right. As you can probably imagine, it was a very difficult time when Sydney first came to live with me. She was lost and very confused; she couldn't understand why her mummy and daddy had left her all alone. I tried to make it as easy as I could for her—I said she could call me whatever she liked: Auntie, Freda, anything. She said she was going to call me Fred, and she has done ever since."

"You must be very protective towards her?"

Freda sat back in the chair, and said nothing for the longest moment, but then managed, "You know, don't you? You know I killed him."

"Yes, but I'd still like you to tell me what happened."

"I didn't mean for this to affect Myrtle. I kept hoping they'd realise she couldn't have done it."

"I assume you were trying to protect Sydney?"

"Yes. The day she first met that good-for-nothing was the worst day of my life. She's always been a little wilful; what kid isn't? But once she got together with that piece of scum, she changed completely. She started drinking heavily and I'm sure she was taking other stuff too. And the way she acted when she was with him—it made me ashamed of her."

"Did you talk to her about it?"

"Of course I did, but she wouldn't listen. She thought the sun shone out of his backside. She couldn't see him for what he was. I was terrified of where it might all end. I kept expecting a call to tell me Sydney had taken an overdose. Or that he'd beaten her up. He was violent, you know."

"Did you send the text message to Rob from Sydney's phone?"

"Yes, I knew he'd never come to talk to me. He thought I was a busybody; he'd told Sydney as much. That's why I came up with the idea of sending him a text from Sydney's phone. It was easy to get hold of it—she was always leaving it lying around. I had planned to get him to meet me at his house, but when I got there, some of his friends were hanging around outside. I still had the key that Myrtle had given me, so I nipped into her house and sent the message from there. I only wanted to talk to him; to try to make him see reason." Freda's laugh sounded hollow. "I should have known better. When I asked him to leave Sydney alone, he laughed in my face. He said he was going to take her back to London with him, and that he'd make sure I never saw her again. Then he lit a joint. I told him he couldn't smoke that filthy muck in the house, and I practically pushed him out into the garden. The more I pleaded with him, the more he taunted me. And then he said that my darling Sydney wasn't the 'good girl' I thought she was, and he began to say the most awful things about her."

Freda began to cry.

"Shall I get you a drink?"

"No, thank you, dear. I just need a moment."

We sat in silence for several minutes before she continued, "I don't remember picking up the poker or hitting him, but the next thing I knew, he'd fallen into the river."

"What happened then?"

"It's all a bit of a blur. I must have caught the bus home, but I don't remember doing it."

"What about the poker?"

"I brought it home in my bag, although I don't recall putting it in there. It's upstairs on top of my wardrobe. Do you want me to get it for you?"

"No. Leave it there for now."

"What's going to happen to me?"

"When you're ready, I'll have to call the police."

"Of course. What about Sydney? Who'll look after her?"

"She'll be okay. I know it's hard to accept, but she's a woman now."

"You're right. I know you are. At least I don't have to worry about what Evans might do to her. What about Myrtle? I'm so very sorry for what's happened to her."

"Myrtle's a tough cookie. She'll be just fine. With a bit of luck, she'll be home before the end of the day."

I waited with Freda until Rosemary Thorne and another police officer arrived. Once Freda had told Thorne that she'd killed Rob Evans, she was taken out to the car by the constable.

"Be gentle with her," I said.

"I've already told you that I don't want you interfering in police business," Thorne snapped.

"I'm not interfering; I'm just asking you to be a little understanding."

"What are you doing here, anyway?"

"I told you. I'm working for Myrtle Turtle. You must remember her. She's the woman you have locked up for a crime she didn't commit. I assume you'll expedite her release now?"

"Once we've been able to verify Mrs Bowling's claims, Ms Turtle's release will be processed by the court."

"And, I'm sure you'll want to apologise to her in person."

"I have to go. You'd better leave too. We'll need to search this house."

I started for the door. "Oh, by the way, no thanks are necessary."

"For what?"

"Doing your job for you."

***

I had an emergency on my hands.

A custard cream emergency, which as I'm sure you're already aware, is the very worst kind.

I'd finished my last packet that morning, and I'd been so busy that I'd totally forgotten to buy some while I was in Washbridge. Unforgiveable, I know, but that's exactly what local convenience stores are there for, so on my way home, I stopped off at The Corner Shop. I was on a mission: Replenish Custard Creams.

But then disaster struck. The shop door was locked and the 'Closed' sign was displayed in the window.

Closed? At five o'clock on a Thursday? How could that be possible? I figured it had to be a mistake, so I hammered on the door. After a couple of minutes, there was still no answer, and I was just starting to wonder if I could justify using magic to break and enter when I was startled by a voice from behind me. It was Little Jack.

"You made me jump. Why is the shop closed?"

"I'm very sorry, Jill. Tomorrow is the final of the Corner Shop Stacking Competition. I spent all last night and this morning preparing my stacks, and I daren't risk anyone knocking them over."

"Won't you lose money by closing the shop?"

"Of course, but that will be far outweighed by the prestige if I were to win."

"But, I'm out of custard creams."

"We'll be open again tomorrow afternoon."

"That's almost twenty-four hours away. I can't possibly

go that long without a custard cream."

"I suppose I could go inside and get you a packet. As long as you don't mind waiting here?"

"No problem, but do you think you could possibly make it a couple of packets?"

"Two?"

"I was thinking more like four."

"Okay. I'll be as quick as I can."

Phew! Little Jack had come through for me. It had taken him a while, but as he'd explained, he'd had to weave his way past numerous elaborate displays. He'd only managed to grab three packets, but that should be enough to see me through the current crisis.

I pulled onto my street, and almost crashed the car when I spotted two clowns outside the next-door neighbours' house. It was Sneezy and Breezy, and they were carrying multi-coloured buckets. At first, I couldn't work out what they were up to, but then the penny dropped.

"Hi, beautiful." Jack met me in the hallway, and gave me a peck on the lips. "Have you had a good day?"

"Yeah, pretty good. What about you?"

"Actually, there was a really interesting case I wanted to tell you about. It involved —"

"Sorry to interrupt, but I need to take a quick shower. I'm sweltered."

"Dinner will be ready in twenty minutes."

"I'll be back down before you know it." I rushed upstairs.

Fifteen minutes later, and fresh from my shower, I

joined Jack in the kitchen.

"You knew they were coming here, didn't you?" He fixed me with his glare.

"Who?"

"Don't give me that innocent routine of yours. You never go straight up for a shower when you get in from work."

"I told you; I was all clammy."

"You saw Jimmy and Kimmy, didn't you?"

"They prefer to be called Sneezy and Breezy when they're in costume."

"There! I knew it! I knew you'd seen them!"

Oh bum! That's what comes of speaking before engaging brain. "I did see them next door. So what?"

"You knew they were collecting their sponsorship money."

"Were they?"

"You know very well they were. Do you have any idea how much you've cost us?"

"*Me*? Why is it down to me?"

"You were the one who put our names down for ten pence a laugh."

"How many laughs did the clownometer register?"

"Eight-hundred and seventy."

"That's outrageous! Are you sure they only counted chuckles as half a laugh?"

"How am I supposed to know? It's not like I can demand an audit, is it?"

"I bet they included smiles too. They weren't supposed to count those. How much did it come to altogether?"

"Eight-hundred and seventy laughs at ten-pence a laugh is eighty-seven pounds."

"I ought to claim some of that back from Kathy. She and Lizzie cost us a good proportion of that. Still, it's for a good cause, I suppose." I sniffed the air. "That smells good. Is dinner ready yet?"

"You do realise you owe me half of the eighty-seven pounds."

"Of course, but I've hardly got any cash on me. I could draw some out tomorrow — unless, of course, you'll take payment in kind." I flashed him my sexiest smile.

"I'd prefer the cold hard cash."

"You don't have an ounce of romance in you, do you?"

Chapter 24

I was munching on toast for breakfast.

"Jack, when I got home yesterday, didn't you start to tell me about an interesting case you'd been working on?"

"You mean before you hid from the money-collecting clowns?"

"I wasn't hiding. I just needed a shower."

"Forty-three pounds and fifty-pence."

"Sorry?"

"That's how much you owe me for your half of the clownathon sponsorship money."

"I told you last night. I don't have much cash in my purse at the moment."

"How very surprising." He grinned.

"It's true. I'll need to call at an ATM today. So, are you going to tell me about this interesting case you were working on or not?"

"We caught a serial burglar who's been eluding us for over a year."

"That's brilliant. I solved a murder and helped to close down a network that was peddling contaminated blood, which was responsible for killing a number of vampires. And I rescued a couple who'd been trapped in a 'world generator' spell. Oh yeah, and I got to ride on a dragon's back. That was pretty cool. Anyway, you were telling me about the burglar?"

"It doesn't matter. It wasn't really all that interesting."

***

Class five-gamma were a challenging bunch. They were

in their final year before graduation, and were difficult to control at the best of times. It didn't help that I'd turned up without a lesson plan, so I'd been forced to throw the floor open to suggestions for topics to discuss.

"Miss!" Sandra Sycamore, who was seated on the front row, thrust her hand up. "Miss!"

"Yes, Sandra?"

"What would you say is the best way to get a human husband?" Several of her classmates laughed, but Sandra was undeterred. "Are those dating agencies worth the money?"

"I don't think you should be concerning yourself with that just yet. It would be much better to focus on your career first."

"How did you meet your husband, Miss?" Veronica Reedmore called out.

"Jack and I met through our work. I'm sure you all already know that I work as a private investigator in the human world. Jack is a detective."

"Was it love at first sight, Miss?"

"Not exactly. For a long time, we didn't get along at all."

"Did you ever try any of the dating agencies that specialise in matching witches with humans?" Sandra Sycamore wasn't letting the subject drop.

"No, but I have done some work for one of them."

"Which one, Miss?"

"Love Spell, but I don't really think this is an appropriate subject for discussion in class. Does anyone else have any other suggestions for topics we can cover?"

Grover Grey's hand shot up.

"Yes, Grover?"

"I heard that you talked to a dragon, Miss. Is that true?"

"I did. Her name is Sybil and she has a lovely little baby called Cora."

"How come you can talk to dragons, Miss?"

"I'm not sure. I don't seem to be able to talk to all of them. When a destroyer dragon was trying to kill me, he didn't seem very interested in chatting. From what I can make out, not all witches and wizards can talk to animals, and even those who can, can't necessarily talk to all of them."

"Do you have any pets, Miss?" Carl Bestwick said.

"I have a cat named Winky. He's called that on account of his having only one eye."

"Is he cute, Miss?" Veronica asked.

"Winky is many things, but no one could ever accuse him of being cute."

"Does he talk to you?"

"All the time. Unfortunately." I checked my watch. "Only a couple of minutes to go. One last topic, anyone?"

"Are the rumours true about the headmistress, Miss?" Corinne Daylight called out.

"What rumours would they be?"

"We've heard that she might be retiring."

I'd heard the same rumours, but I didn't think it was my place to discuss it with the pupils.

"I wouldn't take any notice of rumours." Just then, the bell which marked the end of lesson, came to my rescue. "Okay, off you go."

***

From the classroom, I went straight to the office of the

headmistress.

"Come in!"

"Morning, Ms Nightowl."

"Morning, Jill. How did today's lesson with five-gamma go?"

"Okay, thanks."

"I've been very impressed by the amount of preparation you've done for your lessons. What topics did you cover today?"

"Oh, err — mainly career related."

"Excellent. A good proportion of our students will end up working in the human world, so that kind of information will be invaluable to them." She walked over to the window and looked out. "You're probably wondering why I wanted to speak to you today."

"I am curious. Nothing bad, I hope?"

"I suppose that depends on your point of view." She turned around to face me. "I'm sure you will already have heard the rumours about my retirement?"

"No," I lied.

"It's alright, Jill. I know it's common knowledge in the staff room."

"I did hear something, but I dismissed it as tittle-tattle."

"Actually, it's true. I haven't been in the best of health for some time now."

"I'm sorry to hear that. I had no idea."

"I've done my best to keep it hidden from the staff and pupils, but recently it has been getting more and more difficult to fulfil my duties, so it's time for me to step down."

"I for one will be really sorry to see you leave."

"It's very kind of you to say so."

"Have they appointed your successor yet?"

"Actually, that's the reason I wanted to speak to you today. My replacement will be a wizard by the name of Cornelius Maligarth. I had hoped that I might be involved in the recruitment process, as my predecessor was in mine, but that hasn't happened. He was appointed by the governors without any reference to me whatsoever."

"Have you met him?"

"I have, and I'm sorry to say that I didn't like what I saw."

"Why is that?"

"I wish I knew. I'm not usually one to make snap judgements, but I disliked him at first sight. And the more I spoke to him, the more convinced I became that there is something not quite right about our Mr Maligarth."

"Have you expressed those concerns to the governors?"

"I've tried to, but they seem to have fallen under his spell. They won't have a bad word said against him."

"What do you know about his background?"

"That's the most worrying aspect. After meeting him, I decided to do some research in the hope that I'd find details of a glowing academic record that would put my mind at ease."

"I take it you didn't?"

"That's just it. There's no record of Cornelius Maligarth anywhere."

"Nothing?"

"Nothing at all."

"Isn't that rather strange?"

"Unprecedented, I'd say. It's as though he never existed until now."

"I understand your concern, headmistress, but now that

the governors have made their decision, there's not a lot you can do, is there?"

"There is one thing. Would you come with me, please?" She walked to the back of the office and stopped in front of one of the many bookcases. "Watch carefully." She pressed the spine of a book titled: The Myth and Magic Yearbook. As she did that, the bookcase slid to one side.

"Another secret passageway?"

"Yes, but this one is known only to the head of the school. Its existence is passed on from one head to the next."

"Why are you showing me, then?"

"You'll see. Please follow me, Jill."

The passageway was cold, narrow and dark— illuminated only by a series of small gas lights mounted on the wall. We walked for a few metres then came to a stone spiral staircase. After a long, steep descent, we reached the bottom, and found ourselves in a large, dimly lit room, which was little more than a cave cut from the rock. The room was empty except for a circular plinth in the very centre.

"Where are we, headmistress?"

"Deep below the school. This is the room of shadows. I was brought here on my first day in the job by the previous headmaster, Laurence Runemore, a great man and a renowned scholar. Come over to the plinth, please, Jill. Do you see the letters engraved around the edge?"

I nodded.

"I want you to take note of what I'm about to do. It's essential that you commit to memory the precise sequence I use."

When she touched the letter 'V', it illuminated for a few

seconds. She then went on to press four more letters before taking two steps back from the plinth. I was about to ask what this was all about when the centre of the plinth slid slowly to one side, to reveal a bronze cube.

"What is that?"

"It's called The Core."

"What's it for?"

"I'm not sure exactly, but I was given to believe that if it ever fell into the wrong hands, it could be catastrophic for the sup world."

"How did it come to be here?"

"I assume you know that this building once belonged to Charles Wrongacre?"

"Yes."

"It seems that he stole it from his arch-enemy, Braxmore. It's been here ever since. The only people who know of its existence are the heads of this school."

"Past and present, I assume?"

"All of the ex-heads are now dead. That leaves just me, and I don't expect to be around for very much longer. That's why it's essential I pass on this information now."

"I'm still not sure why you're telling *me*?"

"Under normal circumstances, my successor would be the one standing where you are now, but I simply do not trust Maligarth. I'm afraid if I share this secret with him, something very bad may happen, but I cannot go to my grave without first telling someone—someone I trust. I'm sorry to burden you with this responsibility, Jill, but I don't know who else to turn to."

"I don't mind. I'm just not sure what I'm supposed to do."

"It is possible I may have misjudged the new

headmaster. You'll still be at CASS long after I've left, so you'll be able to form your own opinion of him. If you conclude that my mistrust in Maligarth was unwarranted, you should share this secret with him."

"That's a big responsibility."

"I realise that, and I'm sorry to drop this on you, but I felt I had no choice. Are you prepared to take it on?"

"Of course I will."

***

My head was still spinning, with everything the headmistress had told me, when I magicked myself back to Washbridge. I hoped that her concerns about the new headmaster would prove to be unfounded, so that I could pass on the secret of The Core sooner rather than later.

Mrs V had a follow-up dental appointment, to replace a damaged filling, so I expected the outer office to be deserted. Instead, there was a young woman sitting at Mrs V's desk.

"Can I help you?" I said.

"I—err—I'm here to read the meter."

"Which meter?"

"The—err—water meter."

"There isn't a water meter in this office."

"Sorry, I meant the electricity meter."

"Do you normally find the electricity meter in a desk drawer?"

"I was just sitting here until someone came back."

"Why is that drawer open, then?"

"I didn't open it."

"Could I see your ID, please?"

She took a card from her pocket and handed it to me.

"This is clearly a fake."

"It isn't. Honestly."

"That isn't even your photo. That's a much older woman."

"I've never looked good in photographs."

"And your hair, it's not real, is it?"

"Yes, it is."

"No, it isn't." I pulled off her wig. "And those glasses don't have any lenses in them, do they?"

"No." She took them off and placed them on the desk. "I'm sorry. I didn't want to do this."

"I assume you're from the crocheters?"

"How did you know?"

"Just a wild guess."

"Marjorie, that's the woman in the photo, was supposed to do this, but she's gone down with food poisoning. I told them I'd be no good at it; I've never been able to lie. Are you going to call the police?"

"Have you stolen anything?"

"No, of course not."

"Have you read Mrs V's notes for the knitters' conference?"

"I couldn't find them. I was still looking when you came in."

"No harm done, then, I suppose."

"Aren't you going to have me arrested?"

"No, you're free to go."

"Thank you so much." She grabbed her fake ID card, false glasses and her wig, and then bolted for the door.

Before I could go through to my office, Mrs V walked

in. "Who was that crazy woman who just rushed out of here?"

"She was here to read the electricity meter."

"Are you sure she wasn't a spy after my conference notes?"

"I think you're getting a little paranoid, Mrs V."

***

Myrtle Turtle paid me a visit that afternoon.

"I have to say, Myrtle, you're looking remarkably well considering your ordeal."

"I've been through much worse. I wanted to stop by and thank you for getting me out of there."

"My pleasure. I'm sorry it took as long as it did."

"Don't worry about it. I made a few useful connections while I was inside. What tipped you off to Freda?"

"I'd like to say it was great detective work, but to be honest, it was mostly luck. I knew she was one of the few people who had a key to your house, and when I discovered she was Sydney's aunt, I just put two and two together."

"I feel bad for Freda."

"That's very generous of you, considering she allowed you to take the fall for her."

"I'm convinced she would have come forward eventually. I think she was hoping that I might be released anyway."

"I'm afraid she's likely to face a long stretch inside."

"It's a tragedy. Fundamentally, she's a good woman."

"She did kill a man."

"I know, and I'm not trying to excuse what she did, but

I do understand it. That young woman was like a daughter to her. It must have been terribly painful to see what she was becoming under the influence of that scumbag, Evans."

"What do you think will happen to Sydney?"

"I don't know. Although they'd drifted apart recently, she has relied on Freda for most of her life. I went to see Sydney before I came here, and told her she could call on me if she needed any help."

"That was very generous of you. What did she say?"

"She told me to do one." Myrtle smiled. "Maybe she'll feel differently in a week or two. We'll see."

After I'd seen Myrtle out, I went back to my desk, and found a white envelope lying on it. It was addressed to me, and I recognised the paw-writing.

"What's this, Winky?"

"Open it, and you'll find out." He was on the sofa, washing his paws.

"You're invoicing me for the cost of the new blinds?"

"Yes, and you'll note that I haven't included any mark-up. I'm generous like that."

"You offered to pay for those blinds. There was no discussion about me having to pay you back."

"That's when I was trying to keep hold of Crystal. Now that she's dumped me for Bruiser, I don't see why I should foot the bill to refurbish *your* office. Don't worry, though, you can let me have it by the end of the week."

"Today is Friday. It *is* the end of the week."

"You'd better get down to the ATM then."

ALSO BY ADELE ABBOTT

The Witch P.I. Mysteries
(A Candlefield/Washbridge Series)

Witch Is How... (Books #25 to #36)
Witch is How Things Had Changed
Witch is How Berries Tasted Good
Witch is How The Mirror Lied
Witch is How The Tables Turned
Witch is How The Drought Ended
Witch is How The Dice Fell
Witch is How The Biscuits Disappeared
Witch is How Dreams Became Reality
Witch is How Bells Were Saved
Witch is How To Fool Cats
Witch is How To Lose Big
Witch is How Life Changed Forever

Susan Hall Investigates
(A Candlefield/Washbridge Series)
Whoops! Our New Flatmate Is A Human.
Whoops! All The Money Went Missing.
Whoops! Someone Is On Our Case.

Web site: AdeleAbbott.com
Facebook: facebook.com/AdeleAbbottAuthor
Instagram: #adele_abbott_author

87639378R00153

Made in the USA
San Bernardino, CA
06 September 2018